Alison Roberts lives in Christchurch, New Zealand, and has written over sixty titles for Mills & Boon® Medical Romance™. As a qualified paramedic she has personal experience of the drama and emotion to be found in the world of medical professionals, and loves to weave stories with this rich background—especially when they can have a happy ending.

When Alison is not writing you'll find her indulging her passion for dancing or spending time with her friends (including Molly the dog) and her daughter Becky, who has grown up to become a brilliant artist. She also loves to travel, hates housework and considers it a triumph when the flowers outnumber the weeds in her garden.

Books by Alison Roberts

A Little Christmas Magic
200 Harley Street: The Proud Italian
From Venice with Love
Always the Hero
NYC Angels: An Explosive Reunion
St Piran's: The Wedding
Maybe This Christmas...?
The Legendary Playboy Surgeon
Falling for Her Impossible Boss
Sydney Harbour Hospital: Zoe's Baby
The Honourable Maverick

**Visit the author profile page at
millsandboon.co.uk for more titles**

For Annie, Carol and Linda—who will always
make Melbourne a very special place to visit for me.
Love you all xxx

MIDWIVES ON-CALL

Midwives, mothers and babies—
lives changing for ever...!

**Over the next four months enter the magical world
of the Melbourne Maternity Unit and the exceptional midwives there,
delivering tiny bundles of joy on a daily basis.
Now it's time to find a happy-ever-after of their own...**

In April, gorgeous Greek doctor Alessi Manos is determined to charm the
beautiful yet frosty Isla Delamere...but can he melt this ice queen's heart?

Just One Night? by Carol Marinelli

And when Dr Oliver Evans's estranged wife, Emily, crashes back into his
life, old passions are reignited. But brilliant Dr Evans is in for a surprise...
Emily has two foster children!

Meant-To-Be Family by Marion Lennox

In May, midwife Sophia Toulson and hard-working paramedic
Aiden Harrison share an explosive attraction...but will they overcome
their tragic pasts and take a chance on love?

Always the Midwife by Alison Roberts

And hotshot surgeon Tristan Hamilton's passionate night with
pretty student midwife Flick has unexpected consequences!

Midwife's Baby Bump by Susanne Hampton

In June, free-spirited locum midwife Ally Parker meets top GP and
gorgeous single dad Flynn Reynolds. Is she finally ready to settle down
with a family of her own?

Midwife... to Mum! by Sue MacKay

And when beautiful redhead Phoebe Taylor turns up on ex-army medic
Ryan Matthews's doorstep there's only one thing keeping them apart:
she's his best friend's widow...and eight months pregnant!

His Best Friend's Baby by Susan Carlisle

Finally, join us **in July**, when brooding city surgeon Noah Jackson
meets compassionate Outback midwife Lilia Cartwright.
Could Lilia be the key to Noah's locked-away heart?

Unlocking Her Surgeon's Heart by Fiona Lowe

And renowned English obstetrician Darcie Green might think playboy
Lucas Elliot is nothing but trouble—but is there more to this gorgeous doc
than meets the eye?

Her Playboy's Secret by Tina Beckett

**Experience heartwarming emotion and pulse-racing drama in
Midwives On-Call
this sensational eight-book continuity
from Mills & Boon® Medical Romance™**

**These books are also available in eBook format
from www.millsandboon.co.uk**

MIDWIVES ON-CALL

Welcome to Melbourne Victoria Hospital—
and to the exceptional midwives who make up
the Melbourne Maternity Unit!

These midwives in a million work miracles
on a daily basis, delivering tiny bundles of joy
into the arms of their brand-new mums!

Amidst the drama and emotion of babies
arriving at all hours of the day and night, when
the shifts are over, somehow there's still time
for some sizzling out-of-hours romance...

Whilst these caring professionals might come
face-to-face with a whole lot of love in their
line of work, now it's their turn to find
a happy-ever-after of their own!

Midwives On-Call

*Midwives, mothers and babies—
lives changing for ever...!*

Dear Reader,

One of the perks of being a writer is the joy of including things that are special to me in my stories. Or exploring things that have always intrigued or inspired me.

I got to do this a lot in Aiden and Sophia's story for the *Midwives On-Call* continuity, and that made it a real joy to write.

I adore Melbourne. I've spent a lot of time there in the last decade or so, because it's home to some of my very best friends and my daughter has been living there for the last three years. So I got to include places like the Southbank in the central city and Queenscliff—which isn't part of the city but is gorgeous and *so* worth a day trip if you're ever lucky enough to be spending time in Melbourne. I even gave one of my friends (and her dog) a cameo appearance in the Queenscliff chapter! :)

I also got to learn a lot more about Murderball, or wheelchair rugby, and I find that totally inspiring. Throw in some babies, a gorgeous motorbike paramedic for a hero and a 'three dates' rule that's begging to be broken and it's no wonder I had so much fun writing this book.

I hope you have just as much fun reading it.

With love

Alison xxx

ALWAYS THE MIDWIFE

BY
ALISON ROBERTS

First published in Great Britain 2015
by Mills & Boon, an imprint of Harlequin (UK) Limited,
Eton House, 18-24 Paradise Road, Richmond, Surrey, TW9 1SR

© 2015 Harlequin Books S.A.

Special thanks and acknowledgement are given to Alison Roberts
for her contribution to the *Midwives On-Call* series

ISBN: 978-0-263-25800-4

Ha ... ural,
rer ... wn in
su: ... s conform
to ... n.

Pr
by

CHAPTER ONE

THE BLIP OF the foetal heart monitor had definitely slowed down. Her decision might be a no-brainer but Sophia knew it wasn't going to be popular.

'I'm sorry,' she told her patient, 'but I'm not happy with the way things are going. We need to get you to hospital.'

'No-o-o...' First-time mother Claire Robinson had her heart set on a home birth. 'You said I'm almost fully dilated. It can't be much longer.'

'You're exhausted, sweetheart. Every contraction is harder for you and things are slowing down.' She still had the hand-held Doppler against the distended abdomen of the pregnant woman. 'Can you hear that the baby's heartbeat has slowed down, too? It's a sign that baby is getting distressed.'

'What does that mean?' Claire's husband, Greg, was looking pale and anxious. 'Is the baby in danger? Is *Claire* in danger?'

'No.' Sophia hastened to reassure them both. 'But that's what I want to make sure isn't going to happen. The labour hasn't progressed quite the way we wanted and...' How could she tell these parents-to-be, without scaring them, that it was her instinct that something wasn't right that was making the transfer seem urgent? 'Let me make a call and see how far away an ambulance might be.'

The call was answered instantly.

'My name is Sophia Toulson,' Sophia said. 'I'm a midwife with the Melbourne Maternity Unit at the Victoria. I'm at a planned home birth...' She moved away from the young couple, lowering her voice as she gave the address details and then voiced her concerns.

'An ambulance is probably fifteen minutes away,' the dispatcher told her. 'But we do have a SPRINT guy in your locality.'

'SPRINT?'

'Single Paramedic Response and Intervention. An intensive care paramedic on a motorbike.'

'I think we just need the transport,' Sophia said. 'It's not an emergency...' But she could hear the note of doubt in her own voice. An exhausted first-time mother and a stalled labour. The potential for an emergency was there. Was that why alarm bells had started ringing?

'I'll change the plan,' Claire offered desperately, as Sophia ended the call. 'I'll have more pain relief than the gas. You can rupture the membranes. Whatever it takes...' She was sobbing now. 'We don't want to have our baby in a hospital...'

'I know.' Sophia smoothed damp strands of hair back from Claire's face. 'But you know what the really important thing here is?'

She didn't wait for a response. Greg was perched on

the end of the bed, holding Claire in his arms as she lay back against him. She caught his gaze and then Claire's.

'My job is to keep both you and baby safe. At the end of the day, the only thing that matters is that you get to hold your healthy baby in your arms. I promise that where the delivery happens is not going to take away even the tiniest bit of joy that moment's going to give you.'

A joy that Sophia might never be able to experience herself but that didn't mean she couldn't share it happening for others. It was precisely why she'd chosen this profession. Why she loved it so much. And why she was so passionate about doing whatever it took to ensure a happy outcome.

'That's all I want,' Greg said, his voice cracking. 'For you both to be okay. We always said that we'd go to the hospital the minute we were worried about anything.'

'But I'm not worried. I'm just so tired… Oohhh…' Claire's face scrunched into lines of pain.

'Another contraction?' Sophia reached for the Entonox mouthpiece. 'Here you go. Deep breaths…'

The loud rap on the door made her jump. Surely the ambulance hadn't arrived this quickly?

'Shall I go?' Greg asked.

Claire spat out the mouthpiece. '*No*—don't leave me… It's.… *Ahhh*…'

Sophia wasn't going anywhere either. The contraction had produced a rush of fluid. Claire's membranes had finally broken. It was a sign that her labour was progressing again but Sophia wasn't feeling relieved. Quite the opposite.

The fluid soaking into the pad beneath Claire's hips had the stain of meconium that meant the baby could be in trouble. And...

Oh, dear Lord...yes...that was a loop of umbilical cord showing.

'G'day...' The rich, deep voice came from behind her. 'I let myself in. Hope that's okay.'

Sophia looked up. The man was wearing a high-vis heavy-duty jacket. He had a motorbike helmet on his head with the red, white and blue colours of Melbourne's ambulance service and the title 'Paramedic' emblazoned across the front. The chin-guard and visor were flipped up so that she could see his face but she barely registered what he looked like. There was relief to be felt now— that she had professional help in what had just become an obstetric emergency.

'Claire's waters just broke,' she said quietly. 'We've got a cord prolapse.'

'What's that?' Greg was leaning in, trying to see what was happening. 'What's going on? And who are you?'

The paramedic's helmet was off by the time he'd taken two steps closer. 'I'm Aiden Harrison,' he told Greg. 'Here to help.' He was right beside Sophia now. 'Modified Sims position?'

'Knees to chest, I think. Claire? We're going to get you to turn over, I want you on your knees with your bottom up in the air. Greg, can you help?'

'What? *Why?*' Claire was panting, recovering from the contraction. 'I don't want to move.'

'We've got a small problem, guys.' The paramedic had dropped his helmet and leather gloves, along with a rolled-up kit he'd been carrying. He didn't sound stressed. Rather, he made it sound as if whatever the problem was, it was going to be easily remedied. 'Your baby didn't read the rule book and part of the umbilical cord has come out first. We need to take any pressure off it, which is why we're going to let gravity give us a hand. Here...let me help.'

Somehow he managed to make it seem like nothing out of the ordinary to be getting a woman in labour to get into what seemed a very unnatural position, on her knees with her head lowered. Sophia was ready with the Doppler to check the baby's heart rate again.

Aiden listened, his gaze on his watch. 'Ninety-eight,' he said. 'What was the last recorded rate?'

'One-forty.' Sophia ripped open a packet of sterile gloves. In a blink of time, this had become a potential disaster. The baby's oxygen supply was being cut off. 'I'm going to try and ease the pressure.'

'Oh, my God...' Claire wailed. 'What's happening?'

'You're going to feel me inside,' Sophia warned her. 'I'm going to be pushing on baby's head to take the pressure off the cord.'

Greg's face was as white as a sheet. 'How are you going to take her to hospital if she has to stay in that position?' He glanced sideways to where the paramedic had discarded his bike helmet. 'You're not even driving an ambulance, are you?'

'No, mate. I ride a bike. Gets me where I'm needed faster.' Aiden reached for the radio clipped to his shoulder. 'SPRINT One to Base. How far away is our back-up?'

They could all hear the woman's voice on the other end. 'Should be with you in less than ten minutes.'

'Copy that. Make it a code one.' He nodded at Greg. 'Hang in there, mate. We're under control.'

'I'm getting another contraction,' Claire groaned. 'Ohhh... I want to *push*...'

'Don't push,' Sophia warned. 'Not yet.'

She looked up to find Aiden's gaze on her face. A steady gaze but she could see he knew exactly what she was trying to decide and the almost crushing responsibility for making the right choice here.

'The cord's pulsatile,' she told him. 'And Claire's fully dilated.'

Aiden nodded. If they were in hospital right now, an assisted delivery with forceps would be the fastest and safest way to get this baby out. With Sophia using two fingers to push on the baby's head, the cord was being protected and the blood and oxygen supply was still adequate. She knew what she was doing, this midwife. Intelligent-looking woman, in fact, which probably explained the anxiety he could see in her eyes. She had to know exactly how dangerous this situation was for the baby.

Her hand was probably already aching, although Aiden couldn't detect any signs of discomfort. Could she keep this up until they arrived at the hospital? The other option was not to slow down a natural delivery but to try and speed it up. To get the baby out fast enough to avoid potentially devastating complications from lack of oxygen. She was still looking at him and he got the feeling she was following his train of thought.

'She's also exhausted,' she added. 'Labour's been a bit protracted. That was why I called for an ambulance in the first place. I'm not sure...' Sophia bit her lip as her words trailed to an inaudible whisper. She hated feeling indecisive and it rarely happened, but a baby's life was at stake here and there was another option. But if they encouraged Claire to push and she was too tired to be effective, they would have to wait for another contraction and they could end up in a much worse position, with the baby's head cutting off any oxygen supply. The baby could end up with severe brain damage. Or it could die.

The weighing-up process was lightning fast but agonising. Sophia found she was holding the gaze of the paramedic. Light brown eyes, a part of her brain noted. Unusual. It was a calm gaze but it was intelligent. He knew what the issues were. It was also confident. Crinkles appeared near the corners, like a smile that didn't involve a mouth. There was a good chance they could pull this off.

It was Aiden who broke the eye contact. He crouched beside the bed so that he could look up at Claire who had her forehead resting on clenched fists.

'How tired are you, Claire?' he asked.

'She's stuffed, mate.' It was Greg who responded. 'We never thought it was going to be this hard, you know?'

But Aiden didn't seem to be listening. He was holding Claire's frightened gaze now.

'The best thing for your baby is going to be getting born as fast as possible,' he said. 'And we can help but you're going to have to do most of the work. Do you think you could do that?'

'I want to push,' Claire said with a sob. 'But I'm scared.'

'We're here with you. How 'bout we give it our best shot with the next contraction?'

'O-okay. I'll try.'

'Good girl.' He was smiling at Claire now and the mix of approval and confidence in his voice was compelling. Sophia could have felt defensive about having someone else make that decision for her, but instead she was as ready as Claire to put every effort into making this work. She believed it was the right decision. It *would* work.

Who was this knight in shining armour who'd ridden up on a motorbike instead of a horse just as things were turning to custard? This paramedic with his warm brown eyes and streaked, golden-blond hair that made him look like a surfer.

When the next contraction was due a couple of minutes later, they turned Claire onto her back again and Sophia released the pressure holding the baby's head away from the cervix and the cord. The clock was ticking from that moment on and the three of them, Aiden, Sophia and even Greg—who couldn't help but catch the urgency—coached Claire into giving everything she had. And then a bit more.

'You can do it,' Aiden told her firmly. 'Push, push, push. Keep going. *Push.*'

'Crowning,' Sophia confirmed. 'Keep going, Claire.'

'You're doing great,' Aiden continued. 'But don't

stop. We can't wait for another contraction. This is it. *Push…*'

'*Can't…*' The groan was agonised.

'Yes, you can. You *are* doing it. You're awesome… One more push, that's all we need.'

Good grief, this man had the most amazing voice. Sophia could feel her own abdominal muscles clenching. *She* wanted to push—how ridiculous was that?

'Oh, my God…' Greg's voice was choked. 'I can see him, Claire. Our baby.'

Sophia could see him, too. Could touch and help him into the world, but she'd lost track of how many minutes it had taken since the blood and oxygen supply had been cut off by the pressure of the baby's head and body on the prolapsed umbilical cord.

The baby was limp and blue. It looked lifeless.

Her heart sank like a stone. This had been the wrong decision, then, to let imminent labour progress instead of stalling it and trying to get Claire to hospital before she delivered. This was her patient and her responsibility. How could she have allowed this man she'd never even met before to come in and take charge the way he had? It would be unthinkable to lose a baby like this.

But the motorbike-riding paramedic was by her side, with a kit unrolled and resuscitation gear at the ready and she hadn't yet lost faith in the calm confidence he displayed.

A tiny bag mask to deliver oxygen. Fingers that looked so large against a fragile chest delivering compressions that were gentle but effective.

'Come on, little guy. You can do it. You're gonna be fine...'

The words sounded incongruously casual but Sophia could see the intense concentration in the paramedic's eyes. The fierce determination to save a tiny life.

And there was movement. A gasp as lungs expanded for the first time. A warbling cry. Skin colour that was changing from a deathly blue to a much healthier pink. Arms and legs beginning to stir.

'Hey...welcome back, little guy.' Aiden's hands cupped the baby to gently lift and place the newborn boy against his mother's skin. Both Claire and Greg had tears streaming down their faces. There was an overpowering sense of both relief and joy but fear hadn't been banished yet.

Sophia was watching anxiously. With the level of resuscitation needed, the baby would have still been under intense monitoring in a clinical setting, not being held and touched like this by his parents.

And then Aiden's gaze shifted away from the infant.

'Apgar score nine at five minutes,' he murmured. She could swear there was a ghost of a wink accompanying the report. He knew how anxious she was and he wanted her to know that he was still doing his job—that the baby was being carefully monitored. Sure enough, she could see him resting a finger lightly on the baby's upper arm, taking a brachial pulse. She could stop worrying and focus on Claire. She could deal with the delivery of the placenta and check for any tissue damage.

The emergency was over, almost as quickly as it had appeared.

The ambulance would be arriving within minutes and then they'd have the bustle of preparations to transfer the new family to the maternity unit, where Claire and the baby could both be checked by specialists, but this was a gift of time.

Private time in their own home—the place they had wanted to be in to welcome their first baby.

Aiden stepped back. He stripped off the gloves he'd put on to work on the baby and moved to one side of the room, where he propped an elbow on a tall chest of drawers. He was due to go off duty and he had his usual visit to make as soon as he was done but he wasn't going to leave until the back-up arrived and he didn't want to crowd the young parents as they had their first minutes with their newborn.

Besides, he could watch the midwife as she dealt competently with the delivery of the placenta, transferring it to a bowl where she inspected it for any damage that could suggest part of it had been retained. She was tiny, he noticed. Only a bit over five feet tall. Funny that he hadn't noticed how small she was before. Maybe that was because she'd given off the impression of being confident. Good at her job and in control.

She hadn't felt so in control at one point, though, had she? He remembered that almost telepathic communication between them as they'd weighed up the option of whether to try and stall the labour or push it forward.

Her eyes were a rich brown, weren't they? A nice match for her hair, which had an auburn tinge to its dark colour. It was pinned up to her head to keep it out of the way and Aiden found himself wondering how long it would be if it was unpinned. How soft it might feel.

Good grief… Okay, she was pretty cute but there was no need to get carried away.

But then she looked up from her work and her smile told him there was nothing to worry about.

He could feel that smile as much as he could see it. Gorgeous was the only word for it.

Sophia hadn't noticed the paramedic moving to the other side of the room. Had he apparently read the vibes in the room in the same way he'd seemed to ever since he'd walked in the door?

He'd done the perfect thing, anyway, so she followed his example. Any more cleaning up of either mother or baby could wait until the ambulance arrived. This was a time these new parents could never have again and it was precious. She wasn't about to leave the room and Aiden had chosen the spot that was far away enough to be unobtrusive while still being available so it was a no-brainer to move quietly until she was standing beside him.

He acknowledged her arrival with a grin.

'Good job,' he said softly. 'Thanks for inviting me.'

Her breath came out in a huff of laughter. How could anyone make a life-threatening emergency sound like a party? But paramedics were like that, weren't they? They lived for the adrenaline rush and a 'good' job was one that other medical professionals dreaded having to face. She'd met paramedics who came across as cowboys—galloping from one callout to the next and over-eager to show off their skills.

This one rode a motorbike, for heaven's sake. A mechanical horse. And he'd had no hesitation in taking command and encouraging management that had had the very real potential to have ended in disaster.

Except it hadn't, had it? Another glance at the bed was enough to bring a lump to Sophia's throat. The baby lay in Claire's arms, tiny eyes open and staring up at his parents. Greg's fingers were touching the tiny starfish hand of the baby and his head was touching Claire's. They were both looking down, aware of nothing but their newborn infant. They were talking softly, too, counting fingers and toes and doing what all new parents did in the first minutes of sharing the miracle of new life.

They had probably forgotten the presence of their medical team and wouldn't even hear the murmur of other voices but Sophia looked away, unconsciously allowing them a little more privacy.

It was somewhat startling to find that the paramedic was still looking at her.

'Babies are my favourite thing,' he said softly. 'It was a treat.'

For the first time since he'd let himself into the house, she realised how good looking he was. Oh, she'd noticed the brown eyes and the way they crinkled at the corners and the streaky blond hair. She'd been aware of the intelligence and intense concentration his features could advertise. But he was still grinning at her and she was distracted enough from her patient to appreciate the way everything came together. And not just his face. He had a presence that she'd appreciated on a professional level. Now she was getting the full force of it on a very personal level. Was it so overpowering because he was so much bigger than she was?

No...everyone was pretty much taller than her when she could only boast five feet three inches in bare feet and he probably seemed broader because of the jacket he was still wearing but he gave the impression of a large man. A powerful man, yet she'd seen how skilful those hands had been, positioning the baby's head and fitting the mask to the tiny face. How carefully controlled and gentle his movements had been.

It felt like something was melting deep inside her belly.

He wasn't just incredibly good at his job. He'd done it with humour. With an ability to defuse a terrifying situation. With a confidence that had given them all the belief that they could do it and maybe that had been the reason why they had been able to do it.

Her smile felt odd. As if she was offering him something that she had never offered anyone before on such short acquaintance. Something that came straight from her heart.

'It's me who should be thanking you,' she whispered. 'I can't believe I told Dispatch that we only needed transport, not a SPRINT paramedic.'

'I was eavesdropping on the radio traffic. I'd just ordered a coffee not far away.' He grinned. 'Don't suppose it'll still be hot when I go back.'

'I owe you one, then.'

The crinkles appeared around his eyes again. 'Might just hold you to that.'

Were the butterflies dancing in Sophia's stomach

embarrassment? Did he think she was flirting with him? Suggesting a date, even?

If he did, he didn't seem put off. Or any less relaxed.

Maybe the butterflies were there for an entirely different reason. How long had it been since she'd met such an attractive man? One who had impressed her on so many levels?

Not in the last six months, that was for sure. Changing cities and throwing herself into a new job had left no time at all to think about expanding her social life to include men. She was only beginning to gather a new circle of girlfriends.

Not that this one would be interested, anyway. She could hear an echo of his voice. *Babies are my favourite thing...*

She could feel herself becoming tense. Trying to squeeze something tight enough to suffocate those damned butterflies.

Could he sense that, too? A flicker of something she couldn't identify passed across his face.

'Might be hard to call in the debt,' he said. 'When I don't even know your name.'

'Oh...' She hadn't introduced herself, had she? How rude was that? He'd have paperwork to fill in for this job. He would need more details about Claire as well. 'I'm Sophia,' she said. 'Sophia Toulson. I'm a midwife.'

His grin widened as an eyebrow lifted. 'I should hope so.'

The information about their patient she'd been gathering mentally to help him with his report evaporated as Sophia laughed.

Those cute eye wrinkles deepened and his eyes

danced. 'Come out with me,' he said softly. 'Sophia Toulson, midwife extraordinaire. Come out with me tonight. I'll take a beer instead of a coffee as payment of that debt.'

Sophia's smile died on her lips.

She wanted to say yes.

She really, *really* wanted to say yes, but she could feel her head beginning to roll from side to side.

'No... I can't... I...' The words followed her smile into oblivion. How could she possibly even begin to explain why she had to say no?

Not that Aiden seemed offended by the rejection. His shrug was casual. 'No worries. Maybe another night.'

And then there was a loud knock on a door outside the room. 'Ambulance,' the call came, along with the rattle of a stretcher's wheels.

The snatch of time was gone and Sophia realised that it would have been better spent starting the enormous amount of paperwork she needed to do to record everything that had happened during the emergency birth.

And then she caught Aiden's glance and, if the same thought had occurred to him, he didn't care—he was happy having spent that time doing exactly what they had been doing. And, suddenly, so was she.

Inexplicably happy, in fact, given that she'd denied herself the pleasure of spending more time in this man's company.

But he'd asked. And, for a blink of time, she'd considered saying yes.

That feeling of connection hadn't been one-sided and that, in itself, was something to feel happy about.

Wasn't it?

CHAPTER TWO

I<small>T MUST HAVE</small> been enough because that happiness stayed with her for the rest of her shift.

In fact, this was turning out to be the best day yet since Sophia had made such big changes in her life, leaving her home town of Canberra to shift to Melbourne.

Word had spread quickly through the Melbourne Maternity Unit about her successful management of an obstetrical emergency in the community. With its international reputation for excellence, the MMU attracted the best in the field but this case was earning her congratulations from every quarter.

Alessandro Manos, who headed the neonatal intensive care unit, had been the specialist called to check the baby and he'd been thorough.

'There's no sign of any complications from oxygen deprivation,' he told Sophia. 'He's a lucky little boy that you were there to manage the birth.'

She fastened the disposable nappy and reached for the soft sleep suit Claire had given her to bring up to the unit.

'It wasn't just me. I probably would have chosen to

try and delay the birth and get her in here if I hadn't had some expert paramedic assistance. He was...' Oh, yes...there was a definite extra buzz to be found in the satisfaction of a job well done. 'He was really amazing.'

'Who was?' Isla Delamere—Alessi's fiancée—had popped into the NICU. Her look suggested that the only amazing man around there was her husband-to-be.

'The paramedic who helped me through an acute cord prolapse this afternoon.'

'Oh, I heard about that. How's the baby?'

'Perfect.' Was Alessi referring to the baby he'd just checked? His gaze was resting adoringly on his wife as he spoke.

Sophia's smile had a poignant edge. They might have wanted to keep Isla's pregnancy secret for a bit longer but the news had slipped out and there was no way these two could hide how they felt about each other. They were so happy. And why wouldn't they be? They'd found love and were on the way to being a family.

That had been her own dream once.

People probably assumed it still was. That—like most women her age—she was simply waiting to find the right person to make that dream come true. Only her best friend, Emily, knew that there was no man on earth who could put the pieces of her dream back together.

That it had been permanently shattered.

Maybe it was just as well that the baby scrunched up his face and started crying at that moment.

'I'd better take this little guy back to his mum. She'll be missing him and he's hungry.'

'I'll come with you,' Isla said. 'I want to hear more about this paramedic. Was he hot? Single?'

Sophia shook her head as she wrapped the baby in a cotton blanket and picked him up. An image of those unusual brown eyes, somewhere between hazel and chocolate, flashed into her head. She could even see the crinkles in the corners—the smile that had seemed intimate because it was only intended for the person who had the eye contact.

'Hot enough, I guess,' she said lightly. 'But I doubt very much that he's single.' Liar, her mind whispered. He wouldn't have asked you out if he wasn't single. Her voice rose in pitch as it tightened. 'And even if he was, I wouldn't be interested.'

'Why not?' Loved up herself, Isla was keen for every-body to share her happiness. And maybe she'd picked up on the fact that Sophia was being less than truthful. 'Work is where most people find their partners, you know.'

'I'm not looking for a partner.' With the baby, who'd stopped crying for the moment, in her arms, Sophia led the way out of the ICU and headed towards the room where Claire had been taken for assessment. 'And I do go out. I'm going out tomorrow.' This was a good op-portunity to change the subject. 'You're coming, aren't you? To the gardens?'

'For Em and Oliver's vow renewal ceremony?' Isla smiled. 'Of course. I wouldn't miss it. I think every-body from the MMU is going. It's the perfect way for everyone to move forward, isn't it?' she sighed, probably unaware of the way her hand touched her own belly so protectively. 'Em's very brave, isn't she?'

'She certainly is.' Sophia's arms tightened a little around the precious bundle she was carrying, jiggling him as he started grizzling again. They'd all known that Emily's foster-daughter would only have a short life but her death had been gutting. Only last week they'd all gathered in the children's section of Melbourne's botanical gardens to attend the memorial service for little Gretta. So many tears had been shed as the CEO of the Victoria Hospital—Charles Delamere—had spoken so beautifully about how Gretta's short life had touched the lives of so many others.

They'd all been clutching pink balloons that had been released into the sky at the end of the ceremony. The balloons had all held little packets of seeds—Kangaroo paws—all different colours. Apparently they had been Gretta's favourite and Emily had a vision of new plants growing all over Melbourne. It had been a beautiful ending to a very touching ceremony.

'The plan is that later anyone who can will head for the Rooftop for a drink.'

'I heard that. Did I tell you that Darcie's bringing Flick?'

'The midwifery student?'

'Yes. She's due to start shadowing you next week. We thought it would be a good way for her to get to know everyone a bit better. You don't think Emily will mind, do you?'

'It's an open invitation. We all know Em and Oliver and everyone's thrilled that they're back together. The sad bit's been dealt with and this is about the future. It should be a good party.'

'How formal is it?'

'Not at all. You can wear whatever you like. But I did talk Em into buying a new dress and getting her hair done so I don't plan to turn up in jeans myself.'

Emily Evans had been the first real friend that Sophia had made after moving to Melbourne. They'd clicked instantly and it had been Emily who had helped Sophia settle into her new job and home so happily. An evening with a few wines a couple of months into their friendship had sealed the bond when they'd realised how much they had in common. Their journeys may have been very different but the result was the same—they would never know the joy of holding their own newborn infants in their arms.

Had it been stupid to pick this career? Leaving Isla behind, Sophia had a few moments alone, holding Claire's baby boy. This was the part of her job she loved best. The weight of the tiny body that fitted so snugly against her chest. The joy in the mother's face as she handed it over. Watching a tiny mouth latch onto a breast for that first feed...

It was always there, though...that empty feeling in her own arms. The ache in the corner of her own heart.

Emily's journey had been slower. The hope had still been there for all those attempts at IVF and it must have turned to such joy when she'd finally carried a pregnancy almost to term. How devastating would it have been to experience the stillbirth of her son?

More devastating than it had been to wake from an

emergency surgery to be told that you'd not only lost your baby but that your uterus had had to be sacrificed to save your life? There would never be a transition period of chasing an IVF dream to lead to acceptance for Sophia. She'd only been twenty-one but her life had changed for ever that day.

But it hadn't been stupid to choose this career. Yes, she could have shut herself away from the emotional fallout by choosing a nursing career that had nothing to do with babies or children, but that would have only made the ache worse in the long run and at least, this way, she got to share the joy every day of her life pretty much.

Love always came with some fine print about what you were risking but if you never took that risk, you shut yourself off from what life had to offer. Nobody had ever promised that life was easy and she'd seen more than her fair share of heartbreak in this job, but she'd seen far more people reaping the rewards of taking risks.

Look at Em. She'd chosen to love two children who weren't even hers, both with medical conditions. She'd been brave enough to risk the heartbreak she'd known was coming right from the start. Sophia had thought she was being brave, becoming a midwife and working with other people's babies every day, but, compared to Em, she was still hiding from life, wasn't she?

The next half-hour was happy enough to banish any personal reflections as Sophia spent time with Claire and Greg and the baby who now had a name—Isaac.

The first breastfeed was no drama and she left the happy parents preparing to go back home for their first night as a family.

Weaving through the busy, inner-city streets to get back to her small, terraced cottage when she finally signed off duty wasn't enough of a distraction, however. The ache was a little heavier today. Not just the empty ache of not having a baby to hold. There was the ache of not having a hand to hold. Having someone in her life who was her special person.

It wasn't that she wasn't making new friends here. Good friends. It was because she was essentially alone. She had no family nearby. Her best friend was back with her husband. Sophia had no one who was always available to share the highs and lows of life. And a best friend could never take the place of a life partner, anyway. She had no one to cuddle up to at night.

How stupid had she been, turning down that offer of a date with Aiden Harrison?

Why couldn't she be a bit braver?

If only she could turn the clock back to that moment. She could see those dancing eyes so clearly. A mix of attraction and humour and…confidence that she would say yes?

He hadn't been upset by her stuttering refusal, though, had he?

Maybe, by now, he was feeling relieved.

Oh, for heaven's sake. Sophia gave herself a mental shake. She needed to get over herself or she wouldn't be contributing anything positive at tomorrow's celebration. Maybe she needed to take a leaf out of Emily's book and convince herself that the risk of loving was always worthwhile.

Maybe she could even go down that track herself one day and think about fostering kids.

'It's only me.' Aiden let himself into the big house in Brunswick—his usual stop on his way home. 'Where is everyone? Nate?'

A dark head popped out from behind a nearby door. 'We'll be out in a sec, Aiden. The other boys are in the lounge.'

The lounge was a large room and, like all the other rooms in this converted house, it had polished wooden floors. Unlike most lounges, it had very little furniture, however, because the residents didn't need sofas or arm-chairs. The four young men who lived here were all quadriplegics who needed a high level of domestic and personal assistance. The youngest lad, Steve, was only eighteen. Nathan, at twenty-four, was the oldest.

Not that his younger brother intended to live here for long. This was a halfway step—a move towards the kind of independence he really wanted. At some point they were going to have to talk about it and maybe tonight would be a good time. While he hadn't said anything yet, Aiden was worried about the idea of Nate living independently. He himself had a demanding job and he wouldn't be able to drop everything and go and help his brother if something happened. At least here there were always carers on hand and it was a lot better than the residential home he'd been in for the last few years.

Or was the anxiety about the future more like a form of guilt? That he hadn't been able to care for his brother himself when the accident had happened because he'd only been a kid himself?

That it was his fault that the accident had happened in the first place?

That, if Nathan was capable of living in a normal house, he'd want it to be with *him* and then he'd have to take full responsibility. Oh, he'd have a carer to come in a couple of times a day to help with the transfers from bed to wheelchair and for the personal type care of showering and toileting, but what about the rest of the day? What would happen if Nate fell out of his chair or something and *he* was in the middle of a job like that obstetric emergency today?

He wanted his brother somewhere he was protected and surely this was as good as it got? This was like a regular blokes' flat, with a sports programme playing on its huge-screen television and guys sitting around, yelling approval at the goal that had just been scored.

And then he saw what they were watching. Murder-ball. The loud, fast and incredibly aggressive form of wheelchair rugby that Nate was currently passionate about. Two of the other guys in the house were part of a local team and Nate was desperate to make the grade. Physically, he certainly qualified.

Many people thought that quadriplegics—or tetraplegics—were always totally paralysed from the neck down but the repercussions of a cervical injury or illness were as individual as the people who suffered them and they were graded according to whether the impairment was complete or incomplete and by how much sensory and motor function remained.

With the C6 spinal injury Nate had received at the age of ten, he had little movement or sensation in his lower body. Thankfully, the injury had been incomplete so he still had a good range of movement in his upper body and better hand function than many. If he got his strength up, he'd probably be lethal on a Murderball court.

'Hey, Aiden. Wassup?'

'All good, Steve. How 'bout you?'

'This is our game from last week. Wanna watch?'

'Sure. Not for long, though. I promised Nate I'd take him out for a beer tonight.'

The young woman who'd greeted him came into the lounge. With her short, spiky black hair and facial piercings, Samantha was unlike any of the carers he'd come across in the years of Nate's care so far.

'He's out of the bathroom, Aiden. You can help him finish getting dressed if you want.'

Nathan's face lit up as Aiden went into his room.

'Hey, bro...' The hand held up for a fist bump took away any awkwardness of the height difference between the brothers and Nate's lack of hand strength. 'What do you call a quadriplegic on your doorstep?'

Aiden rolled his eyes. 'I thought you'd given up on the quadriplegic jokes.'

'Matt.' Nathan snorted with laughter and then pushed on one wheel of his chair to turn it towards a chest of drawers. 'What do you reckon? Leather jacket or the denim one?'

'Either's good. We're going to a garden bar but it's not cold out. Want a hand?'

'Nah...I'm good.'

Rather than watch Nate's struggle to put the jacket on unaided, Aiden looked around his brother's room. The poster collection was growing. Action shots of Murderball games, with wheelchairs crashing into each other and flipping sideways and the occupants only staying with them because they were strapped in.

He waved a hand at the posters. 'You could get really injured doing that stuff, you know.'

'Nah.' Nathan had one sleeve of his jacket on but it was taking a few attempts to get his other hand into a sleeve hole. 'A cracked rib or a squashed finger, maybe. Wouldn't be calling you out with any lights or sirens. Hey...any good jobs today?'

'Yeah... Last call was the best. This midwife was calling for transport to take a home birth in to the maternity unit in the Victoria because it had been going on too long. I overheard the call and decided to poke my nose in just because it was handy and things were quiet. Thought I'd just be waving the flag but the minute I walk in, the woman has a contraction and, *boof!* Umbilical cord prolapse and it's turned into an emergency.'

'Wow. What did you do?'

Aiden settled himself onto the end of Nathan's bed. This would need a few minutes because Nate always wanted a blow-by-blow account of every interesting job. If he'd been able-bodied, he would have been a paramedic himself, no question about it. You'd think he'd only be reminded of what he'd never be able to do by hearing about it but he never seemed to get enough of hearing about Aiden's professional exploits.

Or anything else about his big brother's life, come to that. He particularly loved to hear about the women he met and those he chose to date. What they looked like, where they'd gone on their dates and whether they'd stayed the night. He'd been careful how much he'd said about the midwife on today's job because Nate would have picked up on that pretty fast and, for some reason, Aiden hadn't wanted to answer the inevitable questions about how cute she was or whether she was single and, if so, why hadn't he asked her out yet?

Nate was so sure that someone was going to come along one day who would make him break his three-dates rule. Aiden was just as sure it would never happen.

If he couldn't take responsibility for his own brother's well-being, why the hell would he make himself responsible for anyone else? He didn't even own a dog, for heaven's sake, and he'd chosen a medical career where he generally never had to see his patients more than once.

Aiden Harrison was only too well aware of his limitations when it came to relationships and he'd found the perfect balance. Life was good. And it would continue to be good as long as Nathan didn't insist on putting himself at risk. Yes…tonight was the night for having a serious talk about the future.

'Let's go.' He matched the invitation with movement, standing up and opening the extra-wide door so that Nathan could manoeuvre his wheelchair into the hallway.

'Is it okay if Sam comes too?'

'Huh?'

'Samantha. You know…my carer? I asked her if she'd

like to come out and have a beer with us and she was keen. There's plenty of staff on tonight so it's no problem.'

'I...ah...' Was he going to be playing gooseberry while his brother was having a *date*?

Surely not.

But *why* not? He knew better than anyone that a disability didn't change who you were and his brother was an awesome guy. Why wouldn't a girl be smart enough to realise that? He had to admit it was a disturbing thought, though. What if Nathan fell in love and got his heart broken? Maybe a man-to-man talk about how well the three-dates rule worked needed to take priority over the talk about how risky independent living could be.

Not that either of those talks was going to happen tonight.

'Sure,' he heard himself saying, as though it was no big deal. 'There's plenty of room in the van. Maybe one of the other guys would like to come too.'

'Nope.' Nathan scooted through the door ahead of him. 'I only invited Sam.'

They were in a very different part of the botanical gardens this time. The guests crowded around the couple who were standing beneath the wrought-iron archway on the steps to the Temple of the Winds. The greenery of overhanging trees shaded them from the hot sun of a stunning autumn afternoon and once again Charles Delamere was in place as the master of ceremonies

'Ten years ago,' he told them, 'Emily and Oliver made their wedding vows. Circumstances, grief, life drove them apart but when the time was right fate brought them together again. They've decided to renew their vows, and they've also decided that here, in the gardens that are—and have been—loved by the whole family, is the place they'd like to do it.'

Emily and Oliver exchanged a look that was tender enough to bring a lump to Sophia's throat. She glanced over at Toby, Em's foster son, who was being held by Em's mother, Adrianna. This was a real family affair.

There had been so many tears at Gretta's farewell in the children's playground and there were probably just as many as the couple exchanged heartfelt vows, declaring their love and promising their commitment, but there was real joy this time. An affirmation that the risk of truly loving was worthwhile.

It was contagious, that hope. Maybe there was someone out there for her, Sophia thought. Someone who could see past the fact that she could never give him children of his own. Maybe she could find what Emily and Oliver had. How good would that be?

Something would have to change, though, if she was going to become as brave as Emily. Not that she knew quite what that something was but she was definitely going to give it some serious thought.

And, in the meantime, she could celebrate her friend's happiness. The Rooftop Bar was a good place to be on a sunny Saturday afternoon. Adrianna took little Toby home after a short time but told Oliver and Emily to stay and celebrate with all their friends. She would sort the final packing that was needed before they all went on their family honeymoon to the Great Barrier Reef the next day.

As often happened, the men gravitated together at one point and Sophia found herself sitting with a group of the women she knew best around a deliciously shaded table. Right beside Emily, she impulsively gave her friend another hug.

'I'm just so happy for you, Em. For you and Oliver. You so deserve every bit of this happiness.'

'It'll be your turn next.' Emily's smile was radiant. 'I'm sure of it.'

Isla overheard the comment. She was smiling as she refilled Sophia's glass with champagne. 'Good timing that she's met that hot paramedic, then, isn't it?'

'What?' Emily's jaw dropped. 'How come I haven't heard about this? Who is he?'

'Nobody,' Sophia muttered. 'Just a guy that turned up for that cord prolapse job yesterday.'

'And he's gorgeous,' Isla added. 'Soph said so.'

'I said he was good at his job, that's all.'

'She couldn't stop talking about him.' Darcie Green had joined them. 'I can vouch for that.'

Emily's sideways glance was significant. 'Just remember what I told you,' she said, raising her glass. 'You don't have to marry the guy. Just get out there and have some fun.'

'Why shouldn't she marry the guy?' Isla asked, between sips of her tall glass of soda water. 'Have you got something against marriage, Soph?'

'Not at all. I'm thrilled for Oliver and Em. And for you and Alessi. And…' Sophia glanced around the table, trying to distract the focus of attention. 'And what's going on with you and Lucas, Darcie? I'm sure I wasn't the only one to notice the sparks flying at the ball.'

Lucas was the super-hot senior midwife at the MMU and, while the husbands of the women about to give birth were less than impressed with his popularity, there was no shortage of expectant mums keen to become his patients. No shortage of women in Melbourne just as keen to fill another potential role in his life either.

Darcie was an English obstetrician, on secondment to the MMR. She was dedicated to her job and professional enough to have made several people sharpen up at work. Lucas didn't seem to be in that number, however, and the antagonism between them had been noted on the grapevine, but the obvious sparks at the ball had not come across as being between two people who didn't like each other. Not at all.

Not that Darcie was about to admit anything. She shrugged. 'We all had a good time at the ball,' she said, carefully avoiding eye contact with any of the other women. 'But if there was anything serious going on, I'd say it was between Flick, here, and Tristan.'

There was a murmur of agreement amongst the women and more than one knowing smile accompanying the nods.

'I'm sure I wasn't the only one to see you two leaving together,' Darcie continued lightly. 'Just what time *did* you get home, young woman?'

Felicia Lawrence, the student midwife, turned bright red. For an awful moment, Sophia was sure she was about to burst into tears.

Whatever had happened that night was really none of their business. Sophia needed to give her an escape route.

'So you two aren't dating or anything interesting like that, then?'

Flick shook her head with more emphasis than was needed. 'I'm not remotely interested in dating,' she claimed. 'My career's the only important thing in my life right now. Like Sophia.'

'I didn't say I wasn't *interested* in dating.' Sophia eyed her glass of champagne suspiciously. Had she had too much? 'I just...haven't met anybody. It takes time, you know—when you move to a new city.'

'But you've met the hot paramedic now.' Darcie was smiling. 'What was his name? Andy?'

'Aiden.' It seemed to be Sophia's turn to blush now. She could feel the warmth in her cheeks as she said his name aloud. 'Aiden Harrison.'

'Is he single? Did he ask for your number?'

'No.' She bit her lip. 'He did ask me for a date, though.'

'And you said *no*? What were you thinking?'

Darcie and Flick seemed very relieved to have the spotlight turned onto someone else's love life and, for Flick's sake, Sophia was happy enough to take centre stage.

'I'm not sure,' she admitted. 'Maybe I thought he was just being nice. I'd said I owed him a coffee because he'd had to abandon one to come to the job. He said he'd take a beer instead. It seemed—I don't know—a bit of a joke, maybe?'

'Nonsense,' the women chorused. She was gorgeous,

they assured her. Intelligent. Fun. Any guy would have to be crazy not to be genuinely interested.

Emily caught her glance in a private moment. She was the only one who might understand that moment of panic. That dip into a whirl of thoughts that had been spinning for so many years now. The issue of meeting someone you really liked and then agonising over when to tell them. On the first date? Did you say something like, 'Yeah, I'd love to go out with you but you should know that if you want to have kids some time in the future then I'm not the woman for you'? Or did you wait until things got serious and then field the repercussions of someone feeling a bit cheated? Deceived, even.

Yes. Emily's glance was sympathetic. But there was something else there, too. Encouragement?

'What does it matter if it did start out as a bit of a joke?' she said. 'Isn't the whole idea to have fun? To let your hair down a bit and enjoy the best of what life has to offer that doesn't have anything to do with work? It doesn't ever have to be anything serious.'

You don't have to marry the guy. Was that code for 'You don't have to even tell him'?

'How many guys do we know who have no intention of getting serious?' she added. 'They're just out to have fun. We could learn something from those guys.'

'Like Alessi.' Darcie nodded. 'Oops...sorry, Isla, but he was a terrible flirt and nobody lasted more than one night. Until you, of course...'

'Not a good example,' Emily chided. 'But you're right. Soph could use a bit of that attitude and just get out there and enjoy herself with some attractive male company.'

Sophia found herself nodding. And hadn't she just made a silent vow that very afternoon that something needed to change in her life? Maybe she wouldn't have to give too much thought to what that something was.

'Maybe I will,' she said aloud. 'Not that there's anyone around who's offering the company.'

'The hot paramedic did. You're probably putting anyone off asking by sending out *I'm not available* vibes. Change your attitude and they'll be around in droves. You might even meet *him* again.'

Sophia laughed. 'I don't think so.' But she reached for her glass of champagne, feeling lighter in spirit than she had for a long time. 'But, hey…I'll give it a go. The next time I get asked out—especially if it's the hot paramedic—I'll say yes.'

'Promise?' Emily raised her glass to clink it against Sophie's. The other women followed her example and the glasses met in a circle over the centre of the table.

'I promise,' Sophie said.

CHAPTER THREE

HE HAD THE best job in the world, no doubt about it.

Aiden was rolling slowly, the red and blue lights on his handlebars flashing as he eased through the crowds on Southbank. The wide, paved area on the south side of the Yarra River offered spectacular views of the river and city from cafés, restaurants and upmarket hotels.

The gorgeous autumn afternoon had tourists and locals enjoying the exercise, food and entertainment. A juggler had attracted a good crowd and so had an old aboriginal man playing a didgeridoo. Aiden could hear the hollow, haunting notes of the music over the bike's engine. He angled his path to avoid smudging the work of a street artist who was working with chalk and then he could see his destination. Another huddle of people, but they weren't there for entertainment. He'd been called to a woman who'd collapsed on one of the riverside benches beneath the trees.

'I've put her in the recovery position,' a man told Aiden as soon as he'd propped the bike up on its stand. 'I did a first-aid course last year.'

'Good work.' He flipped up the chinguard of his helmet. 'Did anyone see what happened?'

'She was walking around, looking weird,' someone else offered. 'Like she was drunk. And then she sat down and just toppled sideways.'

Aiden had reached the unconscious woman. He stripped off his gloves, tilted her head to make sure her airway was open and then felt for a pulse in her neck. It was there. Rapid and faint enough to suggest low blood pressure. Her skin felt cool and clammy. He shook her shoulder.

'Hello? Can you hear me? Open your eyes, love.'

No response. Aiden looked up. 'Does anyone know this woman? Was she with someone?'

There was a general sound of denial and shaking of heads. Aiden checked for a MedicAlert bracelet or necklace as he ran through the possible causes of unconsciousness in his head. He couldn't smell any alcohol and there was no sign of any head trauma. The woman was young, probably in her early thirties. This could be due to epilepsy or drugs or diabetes. At least he could eliminate one of the possible causes easily. Unrolling a kit, he took a small lancet, pricked the woman's finger and eased the drop of blood onto a testing strip for a glucometer. He also reached for his radio to give Dispatch an update. Whatever was going on, here, this young woman would need transport to hospital.

The glucometer beeped and it was a relief to see that the reading was low. Hypoglycaemia certainly fitted with the limited information he'd been given of her appearing drunk and then collapsing. It also fitted the physical signs of the clammy skin, rapid heart rate and a low blood pressure. Back-up was on the way but it would take time to get a stretcher through the crowds from the nearest point an ambulance could park and Aiden had everything he needed to start treatment.

IV access was the first priority and there were plenty of willing hands to hold up the bag with the glucose infusion. He got the small cardiac monitor out of one of the panniers on the back of his bike as well. It had only been a few days ago that he'd read an interesting article suggesting that sudden death in young diabetics could be due to cardiac problems from electrolyte disturbances.

The glucose infusion was working its magic well before he started attaching electrodes. The young woman opened her eyes, blinked a couple of times and then groaned.

'Oh, no…it happened again, didn't it?'

'I'm Aiden, a paramedic. What's your name, love?'

'Hayley. I…' She looked up at the crowd of onlookers. 'Oh…God…this is so embarrassing.'

'You're diabetic?'

'Yeah…I knew I needed to eat. That's why I came along here. I was heading for the food court in Southgate. It came on so suddenly…'

Aiden could see an ambulance crew manoeuvring a stretcher through the crowd. More people were stopping to stare, wondering what was going on. No wonder the poor girl was embarrassed. The sooner they got her into the privacy of the back of an ambulance, the better.

Checking her blood-glucose levels again could wait until then as well. Aiden kick-started his bike and followed the crew, until he could park beside the ambulance. He needed to fill in his paperwork and he had a feeling that Hayley was not going to be keen to be taken to hospital.

'I don't need to go,' she insisted a few minutes later. 'I feel fine now.'

'When was the last time you had a hypo?'

'A couple of weeks ago,' she admitted reluctantly. 'But before that, it hadn't happened for ages. Over a year.'

'That means your control is becoming more challenging. You need a reassessment.'

'I'll go to my doctor. Soon.'

'It could happen again today.'

'I'll eat. I'll go and get a sandwich right now.'

It took time to persuade Hayley that it would be a good idea to go the emergency department at the Victoria but none of the paramedics were happy to let her go when she didn't have someone with her to monitor her condition. And Aiden had something else that was bothering him.

'Have you thought of wearing a MedicAlert bracelet?'

Hayley made a face. 'It's bad enough having to live with something like this, without advertising it. And have you any idea how much harder it makes it to find a job? People look at you like you've got a disability or something.'

Her words stayed with Aiden as he watched the ambulance take his patient away. He stayed where he was, astride his bike, watching the mill of the people he could still see on Southbank. This wasn't a bad place to park up until he got another call. Central city and covering a patch well away from the nearest ambulance station. A young man in a wheelchair went past amongst the crowd.

There was a disability that couldn't be disguised. And he knew what it was like to attract the intrusive attention of people who felt they had the right to ask personal questions. They'd often been directed at him over the years—as if Nathan's brain didn't work any better than his legs did.

'Why's he in a wheelchair, then?'

'Oh, the poor boy. Can he feed himself?'

'How does he go to the toilet?'

The guilt was always there, welded onto his soul, and the curiosity of strangers turned the screws painfully for Aiden, but Nathan had developed a resilience in his teenage years that had astounded him. He could deal with any situation now with a humour that often shocked the nosy people. Like those awful jokes he kept adding to.

'What do you call a quadriplegic under your car? Jack.'

Despite himself, Aiden found his lips quirking. What did it matter what other people thought? Nathan had it sorted. He was happy. In fact, he was happier than he'd ever been right now. The way he'd been looking at Sam the other night... Was something going on already and, if so, how badly could that end? He needed to have a serious talk with his younger brother. Try and get him prepared for something that would hurt more than public scrutiny or pity.

His radio crackled into life.

'Code One,' Dispatch told him, giving him an address

not far away. 'Twenty-four-year-old female with severe abdominal pain.'

'Copy that.' Aiden tilted the bike off its stand and kicked it into life. He activated the lights and then the siren. Traffic was building up but he'd be able to weave through it fast. He loved a code one response and the freedom it allowed. With a bike, he got way more freedom than an ambulance to break a speed limit or use the tramlines. He just had to be a bit more careful. Hitting tram lines at the wrong angle and the ambulance would have to stop for him instead of getting to the job.

It took less than four minutes to arrive on scene. Another thirty seconds and he was in the room with the young woman who was bent over a chair and groaning loudly.

'It's the fish I had last night. Ohhh.... It *really* hurts and I've been sick.'

Aiden blinked. Dispatch hadn't bothered mentioning that his patient was pregnant.

'How far along are you?'

'Thirty-seven weeks.'

'And how far apart are the pains you're getting?'

'I dunno. It's happening every five or ten minutes, I guess. But I'm not in labour. It's that fish... I knew I shouldn't be eating prawns.'

It took very little time to convince his patient that this was, indeed, labour.

'I'm not going to hospital. I'm having a home birth. Can you call my midwife?'

'Sure. What's her name?'

'Sophia Toulson. Her card's on the fridge.'

The phone in his hand seconds later, Aiden found himself smiling again. It was surprising how strong the hope was that Sophia would be available and able to get here fast.

For his patient's benefit, of course...

Flick was excited. This was the first home birth she had been to since starting to shadow Sophia.

'But what if something goes wrong? Like a post-partum haemorrhage or something?'

'We call for back-up. The Melbourne ambulance service is fabulous. And we're not far from the hospital. In most cases, if there's going to be trouble, we get enough warning.'

'You didn't the other day, with that cord prolapse, did you?'

'No.'

And her pager hadn't warned her that the paramedic on scene had been riding a motorbike. She could see it parked outside Gemma's house.

'Nice bike,' Flick murmured.

'Mmm.'

Those butterflies were dancing in her stomach again. How many SPRINT paramedics rode bikes in the city? It didn't mean that she was about to have another encounter with the man her friends were all now referring to as 'the hot paramedic'.

Except it appeared that she was.

'Hey...' Aiden Harrison was grinning. 'We've got to stop meeting like this. Rumours will start.'

Flick gave a huff of laughter and Sophia gave her

a warning glance before letting her gaze shift back to Aiden, her lips curling into a smile.

'You did say that babies were your favourite thing but you don't have to take over my job, you know.' She moved past him. 'Why didn't you call me when the pains started, Gemma?'

'I didn't think it was labour. I thought I had some dodgy prawns last night because I started getting cramps just after I'd eaten. They went away for a while this morning and then one was so painful I screamed and my neighbour called the ambulance.'

'Contractions are four to five minutes apart,' Aiden told her. 'Lasting about ninety seconds. Vital signs all good. Gemma's been happy to keep walking around.'

'Let's get you on your bed for a minute,' Sophia said. 'I want to check how baby's doing and what stage of dilatation you're at. This is Flick, by the way. Our student midwife. Are you happy to have her assisting? It's very valuable experience for her if she can be hands-on.'

Gemma nodded as she let Sophia guide her towards the bedroom.

'I can stay until I get another call,' Aiden said. 'Unless I'm in the way.'

It was entirely unprofessional to get distracted by noticing how much she didn't want him to disappear. Even worse to take another look at him and find it so hard to look away. Those eyes were just as warm and interesting as she'd remembered, and that smile made it impossible not to smile back.

Oh…help. How long had they been staring at each

other? Long enough for Flick and Gemma to exchange a surprised glance and then a complicit grin.

'It's fine by me if you stay,' Gemma said. *You know you want to*, her tone suggested. 'My mum's on her way but I told her not to hurry. This is going to take ages, isn't it?'

'Let's find out. Flick, get some gloves on and you can examine Gemma and find out what her stage of dilatation is.'

Keeping her voice low, it was possible to use this opportunity as a teaching and practical experience session for Flick.

'Tell me how you'll make the assessment.'

'At two centimetres I'll be able to fit one finger loosely through the cervix but not two fingers. Two fingers will be loose at four centimetres. There's two centimetres of cervix palpable on both sides at six centimetres, one at eight and there's only an anterior lip or a bit left laterally at nine centimetres.'

'And what are you feeling?'

'Nothing.' Flick's eyes widened. 'I can't feel any cervix at all. Am I doing something wrong?'

Sophia smiled as she double-checked Flick's findings, shaking her head at her student, who had been correct in her evaluation. 'You're fully dilated, Gemma,' she told their patient. 'Let's check the baby's position and then get set up. What do you need to do now, Flick?'

'The four Leopold's manoeuvres. First one checks the upper abdomen to make sure it's the baby's buttocks and not the head and then the umbilical area to locate the baby's back and—'

'Can I go to the bathroom first?' Gemma pleaded. 'I really need to go.'

Aiden helped Flick set up for the birth while Sophia stayed close to Gemma. They spread waterproof sheets over the bed and one of the armchairs in the living room and gathered some clean towels. Flick opened a kit and checked the resuscitation gear they carried in case it would be needed.

Aiden found himself glancing frequently at the door, waiting for the reappearance of Sophia and Gemma.

The attraction he'd felt the first time he'd met the cute little midwife had come back with a vengeance. Those lovely brown eyes were so warm and that smile made him feel like he'd just done something outstanding. Something that deserved approval because he'd somehow made the world a better place.

Heck...all he'd done was crack a fairly weak joke. Imagine how Sophia would look at him if he really did something to be proud of.

He wasn't going to let his opportunity slip past. He might have made a note of the number he'd used to call her but that was just her pager service. He was going to ask for her personal number as soon as he got the chance—as long as he didn't get called away first. Who knew how long this labour might take? Gemma was taking long enough just to go to the loo.

And she was being noisy about it, too. They heard a cry of pain. And then another.

And then Sophia's calm voice. 'Could you bring a couple of towels, please, Flick? Lean on me, Gemma...

Yes, that's your baby's head you can feel. Deep breath and give me one good push...'

The wail of a healthy newborn could be heard a moment later and Aiden moved to peer in the bathroom door at the crowded scene. Gemma was still sitting on the toilet and Sophia was guiding her hands to help her hold the slippery baby against her skin. Gemma was sobbing and Sophia looked...as if she was blinking back tears?

'She's gorgeous, Gemma. A dear wee girl... Flick, have you got the clamps and scissors? Gemma, would you like to cut the cord?'

'No...' Gemma shook her head.

Somehow, Aiden had moved further into the small space without noticing and he was now blocking Flick's access to the toilet. Some signal passed between Sophia and her student and Aiden found himself holding the clamps in his gloved hands. He attached one a few inches away from the baby and then another to leave an isolated area to cut. He'd done this before and knew to expect how tough it was to cut through the umbilical cord.

He already felt involved in this birthing scene but then Sophia smiled at him again.

'Can we give baby to Aiden for just a minute, Gemma? I'd like to get you cleaned up and comfortable in bed to wait for the placenta.'

Flick gave him a clean towel and Aiden carefully took charge of the tiny infant, with Sophia's assistance. This was the closest he'd been to her and he could smell the fragrance of her hair. Almost feel the warmth of her skin through the gloves as their hands brushed. And then he looked at the tiny scrunched-up face of the baby and got completely distracted.

The miracle of birth never failed to amaze him but he never wanted the responsibility of one of these himself. The enormity of bringing a new person into the world and trying to keep them safe for ever was overwhelming. As he backed away, carrying the precious burden in his arms, he looked up to find Sophia watching him.

He couldn't read the expression in her face but it struck him as poignant and something inside his chest squeezed hard. But then it was gone. She smiled and turned back to her patient.

'Put your arm around my shoulders and we'll take this slowly. You might find your legs are pretty shaky.'

The five-minute Apgar score was a perfect ten and Aiden returned the pink, vigorously crying infant to his mother. There was no reason for him to stay on the job any longer and watch as Sophia guided Flick to help the baby latch onto Gemma's nipple and begin its first breastfeed.

And then Sophia supervised Flick in attending to the delivery of the placenta and checking it for any damage, and it really was time for him to leave. He stripped off his gloves and picked up his helmet and kit.

Flick was giving Gemma a wash with a hot, soapy cloth and Sophia was putting the placenta into a bag. This was it—the best opportunity he was going to get. He stepped closer.

'I know you were busy last time I asked,' he said

casually. 'But are you doing anything special after
work today?'

Wide, surprised brown eyes met his gaze. 'Not really,'
she said, 'but I won't finish for a while. We usually
spend a few hours with a new mother and make sure
she's happy before we go.'

'Maybe we could meet up later, then?'

Gemma looked up from watching her baby suckle.
'Are you asking Sophia for a date?' She grinned.

Flick was staring at Sophia and seemed to be stifling
laughter. What was going on here?

Sophia tied the bag and stripped off her gloves. Her
cheeks had a rosy glow and she seemed to be carefully
avoiding meeting his gaze. 'It's not about a date,' she
said. 'I happen to owe Aiden a coffee, that's all.'

She made it sound like that was the only reason he
might be interested in taking her out. Aiden couldn't
let that pass.

'Yeah...' he said slowly. 'I'm asking for a date. Would
you like to come out with me this evening, Sophia?'

'Um... I...' Sophia bit her lip. 'Maybe you can call
me later. We're both at work and this isn't, you know,
very professional.'

'I don't mind,' Gemma said.

'And I'm not going to tell anybody,' Flick added. She
looked as if she was trying not to smile. 'Was that a *yes*
I heard there, Soph?'

There was definitely an undercurrent here that Aiden
had no way of interpreting but right then Sophia met his
gaze again and he didn't care about anything other than
hearing her say that word.

'Okay. Yes.' He could see her chest rise as she took a deep breath. 'I'd love to go on a date with you, Aiden.'

'Cool. I'll pick you up about seven? Where do you live?'

'How 'bout I meet you somewhere? A nice bar, maybe?'

So she didn't want him to know where she lived? No problem. When you had a three-dates rule, it was probably better not to intrude too far on anyone's personal space. Aiden named a trendy bar that he knew wasn't too far from the Victoria, guessing that Sophia probably lived reasonably close to where she worked.

'I know it.' She nodded. 'I'll meet you there at seven.'

At six-thirty p.m. Sophia was staring at the pile of clothes on her bed.

It might be a cliché but she really *didn't* have anything to wear. Nothing that would project the image she wanted anyway, which was one of a confident young woman who wasn't the least bit desperate. Who was happy to go out and have a bit of fun but wasn't looking for anything remotely serious.

Something frilly? She didn't possess frills. Something low-cut that would show a bit of cleavage? No. That might send entirely the wrong message about the kind of fun she was after.

What *was* she after? And why was she feeling so ridiculously nervous?

'Oh, for heaven's sake.' Wearing only her jeans and bra, Sophia went to rummage in her handbag for her phone. She would text Aiden and tell him she couldn't make it after all. One of her patients had gone into early labour? Yeah…perfect excuse.

And she wasn't really breaking her promise, was she? She had said yes. She just wasn't going to follow through and actually *go* on the date.

A small problem became apparent the moment she picked up her phone. She didn't have Aiden's phone number, did she?

She had absolutely no way of contacting him unless she fronted up at the bar in…oh, help…twenty minutes.

But there was a message on *her* phone. For a hopeful heartbeat Sophia thought that Aiden might have sent her a message to cancel the date.

No such luck. He didn't have her number either, did he?

The message was from Emily. 'I hear you said yes,' it said. 'You go, girl. And have fun.'

So Flick had spread the word. Her friends would demand details and she was a hopeless liar. Her voice always got sort of tight and high. She'd never be able to make something up and sound convincing.

Gritting her teeth, Sophia marched back into her bedroom. She jammed her feet into knee-high boots, threw on a camisole top and covered it with a velvet jacket. Pulling the band from her hair, she raked her fingers through the shoulder-length waves and spent no more than thirty seconds in front of the mirror, putting on a slick of lipstick.

Then she grabbed her bag and slammed the door of the cottage behind her. She had less than ten minutes to get to the bar but having to rush was probably a good thing. It would give her less time for her stupid nerves to grow wings.

There was no sign of Sophia.

Aiden ordered a beer and stayed at the bar, an elbow propped and his posture relaxed enough to suggest he was thoroughly enjoying his view of the women coming in through the doors. Enjoying the appreciative looks he got in return even more.

Normally, he would be doing exactly that.

So why did he feel…good grief…*nervous*?

A little out of control even?

Maybe it was because he was meeting Sophia here, instead of having picked her up first. What if she didn't show up?

Hey…no problem. There were plenty of very attractive women who seemed to be here unaccompanied by any male friends.

But he hadn't come here to randomly score. He'd come here because he really wanted to spend some time with Sophia.

And maybe the strength of that want was why he was feeling a bit weird. Why this was assuming an importance that it wasn't allowed to have.

No problem. Aiden took another fortifying swallow of his beer. This was only a number-one date. No big deal. If it continued to feel weird, he could just pull the plug and there wouldn't be a number two.

Suddenly, he saw her. Looking small and a little bit lost as she stood near the door and scanned the crowded bar. And then she spotted him and smiled.

The noise of the people around him and the background music seemed to fade away.

The people themselves seemed to fade away. Until there was only himself.

And Sophia.

How weird was *that*?

CHAPTER FOUR

HE WAS THERE.

He must have spotted her the moment she walked through the door because he was already looking straight at her when Sophia turned her head. She'd been worried she might not even recognise him out of uniform but even in a crowd of people there was no mistaking Aiden Harrison.

Her relieved smile faded as she threaded her way to the bar, however. He hadn't smiled back. He'd looked a bit stunned even... Had he been surprised that she'd actually turned up? Or maybe he was disappointed that she had. There was no shortage of opportunities in a place like this. She could feel the gaze of other girls on her as she made her way towards the gorgeous guy standing alone at the bar. Envious glances.

'Hi...' He was smiling now. 'Can I get you something to drink?'

'A white wine would be lovely, thank you.'

'Do you want to have it here or find a table out in the garden? They have live music here tonight so there won't be any room to move in here soon.'

So she'd end up dancing or squashed against him at the bar? Sophia sucked in a breath. 'The garden sounds great.'

There were rustic tables and wrought-iron chairs, flickering candles and the greenery of a rampant grape-vine on an overhead pergola. The last unoccupied table they found in a corner with only two chairs was roman-tic enough to make Sophia hesitate. This was supposed to be fun. Nothing serious.

Aiden put their drinks down on the table. 'Don't know about you,' he said, 'but I'm *starving*. Fancy some nachos or a big bowl of fries?'

That was the right note to hit. They were here for a drink and something to eat and it just happened to be with company. They'd be able to hear the music out here without being deafened. A fun night out.

'Sure. Nachos are my absolute favourite.'

'Mine, too.'

They grinned at each other. They were on the same page and suddenly everything seemed easy. Over the cheese and bean-laden tortilla chips, the conversation was just as relaxed.

'It must be a great job, being a SPRINT paramedic.'

'Best job in the world. I love having no idea of what's coming next or where I'm going.'

'I love being out of the hospital environment most of the time, too. You get to connect a lot more with pa-tients when you're in their own home. Even more when they've had a home delivery. I feel like part of the fam-ily sometimes.'

But Aiden shook his head at that. 'It's the opposite

that appeals to me. I get to ride in, do the exciting stuff and then hand the responsibility on to someone else.'

'Don't you ever follow your patients up and see what happened?'

'I'll talk to the crew that transports them. Or, if I've travelled in with them, I might hang around in the emergency department and see how it's handled from there. Some of the docs are great. If I'm ending a shift, they let me go into Theatre or talk over the results of a CT scan or something. If I can learn something that's going to help me manage better next time, I'm in.'

'You should poke your nose into the MMU some time. You're a bit of a hero up there after that cord prolapse job the other day.'

Aiden shook off the compliment. 'We were lucky.' He raised his eyebrows. 'How's that baby doing? Do you know?'

Sophia laughed. 'Of course I know. I'm still doing daily visits. His name is Isaac and he's doing extremely well. Claire and Greg are over the moon.'

'Good to know. Did he get a thorough neurological check?'

It was Sophia's turn to raise her eyebrows. 'Are you kidding? We've got the best doctors there are. He passed every test with flying colours. He might turn out to be a brain surgeon himself one day. Or the prime minister or something. You'll see him on television and think about what might have happened if you hadn't been there the day he was born.'

'I might have a bit of trouble recognising him.' But Aiden was smiling and Sophia felt...relieved? He did have a connection with his patients that wasn't purely technical. Maybe he didn't want to revel in that connection like she did but it was there—whether he wanted it to be or not.

And the idea of him being a maverick medic who rode around the city saving lives and touching those lives only briefly added to his attraction, didn't it? Gave him a kind of superhero edge?

Oh, yeah…the attraction was growing for sure and it didn't seem to be one-sided. Eye contact was becoming more frequent and held for a heartbeat longer. Their fingers brushed as they shared the platter of food. The butterflies in Sophia's gut danced up a storm as she wondered if he would kiss her at the end of this date.

But then what?

She could hear an echo of Em's voice in the back of her mind. *You don't have to marry the guy. You don't even have to tell him anything. Just have fun…*

Maybe the connection was even stronger than it felt. She could see a flicker in Aiden's eyes that had nothing to do with the candles around them.

'I should warn you,' he said, 'that I'm not looking for anything serious.'

Good grief…was that shaft of sensation disappointment? Or shame even? Was there something about her that wasn't attractive enough to warrant any kind of emotional investment?

His smile suggested otherwise. So did the way his hand covered hers, touching her skin with the lightness of a feather—the fingers moving just enough to sound a deliciously seductive note.

'It's not that you're not absolutely gorgeous,' he murmured. 'But I have rules. One rule, anyway.'

'Oh?' This was confusing. His words were warning her off but his eyes and his touch were inviting her closer. Much closer.

'A three-dates rule.'

'A...*what*?'

'Three dates. I've discovered that's the perfect number.'

'Perfect for what?'

'To get to know someone. To have fun but not to let anything get out of hand. You know...to get...*serious*.'

He made the word sound like some kind of notifiable disease. Sophia's head was spinning. Wasn't this exactly what she was looking for? Fun with a gorgeous guy but within limits. Limits that would mean there was no need to tell him anything about herself that could impinge on the fun. She could pretend there was nothing wrong with her. That she was as desirable as any other young woman who was out there dating. That it was only because of 'the rule' that it wouldn't go any further.

'I love it,' she whispered with a smile.

'Really?' Aiden's eyebrows shot up. His fingers tightened over her hand.

'Really.' Sophia nodded. 'I'm not looking for anything serious either. Three dates sounds like exactly the rule that's been missing from *my* life.'

'Wow...' Aiden's gaze was frankly admiring. 'You're even more amazing than I thought.' He stood up, still holding Sophia's hand, so that she was drawn to her feet as well. 'You do realise that means we'll have to make the most of each and every date, don't you?'

The butterflies had congregated into a cluster that throbbed somewhere deep in Sophia's belly like a drum-beat. She couldn't look away from Aiden's gaze, even when he dropped her hand and raised his to touch her face. A finger on her temple that traced a gentle line around her eye, across her cheek and down to the corner of her mouth. Her lips parted in astonishment at the wave of sensation the touch was creating and it was then that Aiden dipped his head and kissed her.

Right there—in a noisy, crowded garden of a trendy bar. Their corner was secluded enough but it was a long way from being private. Not that the kiss got out of hand or anything. The control of those soft, questioning lips on hers suggested that Aiden was a very experienced kisser. The teasing touch of his tongue hinted at where this kiss could go at any moment. Oh, yeah…it ended far sooner than Sophia would have chosen.

What now?

Would Aiden take her home to his place? Should she suggest that he came to hers?

On a *first* date?

The idea was shocking. Okay, she was doing this to have fun but jumping into bed with someone this fast made it feel wrong. But they only had three dates to play with, didn't they? Did 'making the most of them' imply that they shouldn't waste any time?

But Aiden was smiling again and Sophia had the feeling that he knew the argument she was having with herself.

'Let's plan date number two,' he said. 'And give ourselves something to look forward to.'

'So…how was it, then?'

'What?'

'Date *numero uno* with the cute midwife?'

Aiden shrugged as he looked away from his brother to stare over the veranda railings into the garden of the old house. He upended his bottle to catch a mouthful of his beer. 'Not bad.'

'Score?'

Aiden frowned. Nate loved to hear about his love life as much as his job and he'd always been happy to share the details. He couldn't remember who had come up with the scoring system but it had become a tradition. This was the first time it had occurred to Aiden how degrading it would seem if the women he dated ever knew about it.

Not that he would ever tell them, of course.

But he'd never told any women about the three-dates rule until now, had he? It was a secret, known only to himself and Nate. The astonishment factor of actually sharing the secret with a woman he was on a date with was only surpassed by the totally unexpected way Sophia had embraced the idea.

What was with that? Was there something about him that didn't make him attractive longer term?

The thought shouldn't be disturbing but it was. So was the niggle of doubt that he'd come right out and put a limit on how much time he was going to have with the gorgeous Sophia. How the stupidity of that move had been plaguing him ever since he'd left her at the end of their date with no more than another kiss.

She was...

'That good, huh?' He could hear the grin in Nate's voice. 'Off the scale, was she?'

Aiden merely grunted.

She was perfect, that's what she was. Absolutely gorgeous. Smart. So easy to talk to. And that all too brief taste of her lips...

Man... The way she'd felt in his arms. The way she'd responded to his kisses. He had a fair idea of exactly where their second date was going to end up and he couldn't wait. How, in fact, would he be able to enjoy the day on the beach they now had planned for when their next days off coincided? He would be hanging out to get her somewhere a lot more private. Somewhere they could *really* get to know each other.

But that would mean there was only one date left. And then what?

This had never bothered him before. He'd never even thought ahead like this before.

'Could be the one, then.' Nate was nodding. 'A four-dates woman.'

'No way.'

'Why not?'

'Because I'm not getting into anything serious, that's why.'

'Why not?'

This was getting annoying. Aiden had stopped by after work for his usual visit. He just wanted a quiet beer with his brother, not some kind of interrogation.

'You know why. I'm not interested in getting married or having kids.'

'Doesn't mean you can't have a long-term relationship. Not every woman out there is hanging out to walk down the aisle in a meringue dress or stockpile nappies.'

'They all get to that point at some stage. I know that from painful experience. And the longer it goes on for, the harder it is when you break it off. I'm not going to be responsible for someone else's happiness.'

'Why not?' There was an edge to Nate's voice he hadn't heard before. 'Because you feel you have to be responsible for mine?'

'Whoa...where did that come from?' Aiden glanced over his shoulder as he broke the moment of startled silence. Wasn't it about time for the boys to all roll their chairs into the dining room for their evening meal? Where was everybody else, anyway? In the lounge, watching reruns of Murderball games? If he stepped away from the corner he could probably see through the window and, if there was a game on, he could distract Nate. He had a feeling that he wasn't going to like whatever Nathan was about to unbottle.

'You do, though, don't you?' Nathan swivelled his wheelchair with practised ease and trapped Aiden so that it would look like a deliberate evasion if he tried to step past him. 'You feel responsible for what happened to me and so you think you have to *be* responsible for me for the rest of your life.'

Of course he felt responsible for what had happened. It had been his fault.

Nate was staring at him. He shook his head. 'It wasn't your fault.'

Aiden stared back at him. 'You were too young to remember what it was like. If I hadn't lost my rag and yelled back at Dad, he'd never have come after me. He'd never have knocked you down the stairs and broken your neck.'

The horror of that day as a sixteen-year-old whose life had changed for ever in a heartbeat had never gone. Crouched over the crumpled form of his ten-year-old brother at the bottom of the stairs, his hands had been shaking as he'd tried to hold his phone still enough to call for an ambulance. To stop Nathan moving, even as they'd both heard the dreadful sound of the gunshot that had come from an upstairs room.

Maybe the worst horror had been the relief of knowing that he didn't have to protect Nathan from their father's tyranny any more—the twisted bitterness that had come from blaming an innocent baby for his wife's death.

He'd held Nathan's head still, knowing that moving him could make it worse. And he'd talked to him as he'd crouched there, waiting for help to arrive.

'*I'm here,*' he'd said, over and over again. '*I'll look after you. I'll always look after you.*'

'I remember a lot more than you give me credit for. And you know what? I've had enough of this.'

Nate sounded angry. His clever, brave, determined kid brother was letting his irrepressible good humour go for once. He was angry with him.

Finally. There was a relief to be found in that. He

deserved the anger. He could handle it. He was the one who could still walk. The one who had a job he loved. Who could get out there and kiss gorgeous women. Nate was allowed to be angry about what had happened in his life. The opportunities he would never have.

'It was Dad who pushed me down the stairs. Not you. It's ancient history. Get over it, Aiden. *I* have.'

'How can you say that?' Aiden was shocked. 'You have to live with that accident for the rest of your life. It should never have happened.'

'Oh, get off the guilt train,' Nate snapped. 'Yeah...I have to live with it for the rest of my life. *Me*. And you don't get to feel so guilty about it that you stuff up your own life. I'm not having that put on me, thanks.'

'I'm not—'

'Yeah, you are. You baby me. You're always here, checking up on me. Trying to make life better for me, but guess what? I like my life. I don't need this.'

Aiden stared at his brother. He'd thought he could handle the anger but that was when he'd thought it was going to be about the accident that had wrecked a young life—not about him honouring a vow to look after the only person who'd ever been so important to him.

This hurt, dammit. Enough to make him feel angry right back at Nate.

'I've only ever done what I could to help. You were ten years old.'

'And you're still treating me like I'm ten years old. I'm twenty-four, man. I'm grown up. I've got a *girlfriend*.'

How on earth had this all come out after sharing the news that he'd gone on a date with the cute midwife?

'And there's no way I'm going to play by your stupid three-dates rule.'

So that was it.

'You do know it's stupid, don't you?'

'Works for me.' Aiden's voice was tight. At least, it had.

'I'm going to live by myself one of these days,' Nate continued fiercely. 'I'm going to try out for the Murderball team and if I get in I'll give it everything I've got. I'm going to make the best of my life. I don't want to end up like you.'

'What's that supposed to mean?'

'Shut off. Scared of losing control.'

'People get hurt if you lose control.' Surely Nate knew that better than anyone after what had happened.

'So? That's life.' Nate shook his head. 'Get over it and start having some fun. Like me.' The crooked smile was a plea for understanding. Forgiveness, too, maybe, for saying some hard stuff?

The lump in his throat made it hard to suck in a breath. Okay, he was hurt but, man, his little brother had courage, didn't he? He was so proud of him.

A window got pushed up along the veranda and a dark, spiky head emerged. 'You coming in for dinner, Nate?'

'Sure.'

'You want to stay, Aiden? There's plenty.'

'Nah...I'm good.' He needed some time to think about what had just happened. That his brother had grown up and just let him know in no uncertain terms? Or that he thought he had, anyway. He still needed his big brother, even if he didn't think he did. More than ever, in fact, as he strived for independence. Did he think he could do that without a lot of help? Even if he wasn't welcome, there was no way Aiden could back away from his responsibilities here. He might just have to be a bit cleverer in how he looked after Nate.

'Hey...' Nathan stopped the movement of his chair. He looked back at his brother. He looked a lot younger all of a sudden. Worried. Aiden could see him swallow hard. 'We okay?'

If he'd needed any evidence that his brother still needed him, it was right there in how vulnerable Nate looked right now. Aiden didn't hesitate. 'Sure.'

But it was an awkward moment that could go either way.

Aiden did his best to smile. 'You were right, man. She was off the scale.'

Nate's grin tugged at his heart. 'So she gets a second date, at least?'

'Already sorted. We're going to the beach.'

'Maybe me and Sam can come, too.'

Aiden snorted. 'No way. I only invited Sophia.'

CHAPTER FIVE

MELBOURNE IS FAMED for the ability to produce four seasons in one day with its fickle weather. It was also capable of pulling something astonishing out of its meteorological hat—like a blazingly hot day in April when it could just as easily have been more like winter than summer.

How lucky was it that it was like this for date number two when they had agreed that the beach was a good place to go? Sophia stood on the pavement outside the picket fence of her cottage at the appointed time. She was wearing her bikini as underwear beneath her jeans and shirt and she carried a beach towel in her bag—just in case it was warm enough to swim. The thick jacket she had on over her shirt earned her a few curious looks from passers-by but she was just following the instructions that had come with the plan.

Had her choice regarding the mode of transport been a mistake?

'The van's old and clunky,' Aiden had told her as he walked her home from the bar and they'd planned this date. 'But it does have walls. If you're brave, you can come on the back of my bike.'

'You get to use your work bike at home?'

'No. I've got one of my own. A Ducati. A red one.'

'Red, huh? What colour is the van?'

'White. Boring, boring white.' He wanted her to choose the bike. She wanted to see the approval in his eyes when she made the right choice.

'Then it's no contest, is it? I pick red.'

But her stomach did an odd little flip as she saw the sun glinting on the red metal of the huge bike as it rolled to a halt in front of her.

Or was it Aiden's grin as he lifted the visor of his helmet that was doing it?

He unclipped a second helmet and held it out to her. 'Are you ready?'

Sophia had to suck in a big breath. *Was* she ready? This was about way more than a long bike ride, wasn't it?

Those unusual light brown eyes were doing that dancing thing again. A look that implied mischief. *Fun...*

She reached for the helmet as she nodded and returned the grin. 'I'm ready.'

It was a long ride. Leaving the outskirts of Melbourne behind, they took to the open road, heading south. They bypassed the large town of Geelong and sped towards the point where the harbour met the open sea—the quaint seaside village of Queenscliff.

'It's gorgeous,' Sophia exclaimed as they parked the bike and took off on foot to explore. 'Look at the turrets on that house!'

'We're lucky it's not a weekend. With weather like this, it gets really crowded.'

'You've been here before?'

'It's a great destination when I want to get out on the road and blow a few cobwebs away.'

'It certainly does that.' Sophia made a face as she threaded her fingers into the end of her hair where the waves brushed her shoulders. 'I should have tied this up. I might never get the knots out. I didn't even think to bring a brush. It probably looks like a rat's nest.'

Aiden stopped walking. They were outside the door of a bakery and a woman came out, laden with paper bags. She had to walk around them but Aiden didn't seem to notice because he was only looking at Sophia. He caught her hand and pulled her fingers out of her hair. Then he flattened her hand gently against her head with his still on top of it.

'Forget about it,' he told her. 'You look gorgeous.'

And then he bent his head and kissed her. Right there on the footpath, half blocking the door to the bakery.

Sophia had relived the softness of that first kiss in a bar a hundred times by now. Had conjured up the tingle of anticipation and the curl of desire so many times that she'd been sure she had magnified it out of all connection with reality.

Turned out she hadn't.

This was even better. It still had the restraint that being in a public place required but there was a new depth to it. A familiarity. The knowledge that they both wanted this and it was going to go somewhere else. Very soon.

'*Excuse* me.' The voice sounded annoyed. Breaking apart, they could see why. A young woman with a twin pushchair had no chance of getting past them to the door.

Aiden smiled at the mother as he murmured an apology. He held the door open for her but it was obvious she had already forgiven him.

'No worries,' she said, smiling up at him. 'You have a great day.'

'Oh...' Aiden's glance went over the top of her head, straight to Sophia's. 'I already am.'

The woman turned her head and her smile widened. Her gaze told Sophia exactly how lucky she was. Then she winked and disappeared into the shop. The smell of something hot and delicious wafted out as the door swung shut.

'Hungry?'

'Starving.' Sophia took a step towards the door but Aiden shook his head.

'Bit crowded in there. I've got a better idea.'

He took her across the road to the fish-and-chip shop. A short time later, they were walking down the hill and away from the shops. Aiden held the big white paper parcel in one hand and Sophia's hand in the other. He led her across the railway lines and onto a track that took them to a grassy spot with a view through the trees to the water. The meal was still hot and absolutely delicious. A woman walked past on the track with a dog and then a whole family with a toddler in a pushchair and a small child on a bike, but nobody came to share their patch of grass or even looked their way. It felt as if they were almost invisible.

'This is perfect.' Sophia licked salt off her fingers as she looked away from the pelicans and swans gliding peacefully on water still enough to mimic glass.

'Mmm. I find it pays to put some effort into planning date number two.' Aiden turned away from the view with a smile.

'One of the rules? I'll—um—have to remember that.'

Not that she was likely to remember anything other than the look in Aiden's eyes that she could already recognise as the intention to kiss her. She barely even noticed the colourful cloud of parakeets landing on the fig tree that was shading them as Aiden leaned towards her.

The cloak of invisibility was still around them but Sophia would have forgotten about the rest of the world anyway as soon as Aiden's lips touched hers. Or maybe it was the moment she felt things change as the intensity kicked up several notches. Aiden's hand cradled her head as he pushed her back to lie on the grass. Their tongues danced, the pang of lingering salt a delicious foil to the sweetness of escalating desire. She felt the touch of Aiden's fingers beneath the hem of her shirt, a trail of fire on the delicate skin of her belly, and the heat when it reached her breast was enough to make her gasp into his mouth.

He pulled away with a groan.

'You make me forget where I am,' he murmured.

'You're on date number two,' Sophia whispered back. 'I think it's okay to get distracted. Isn't it?' she added, feeling her eyes widen.

'Yes, but there's a time and place for everything. And

this probably isn't the place for what I'm thinking about right now.'

Sophia's inward breath was audibly ragged as she sat up. She'd been thinking along similar lines and she certainly hadn't wanted him to stop. Anybody could have seen them. Like that woman with her dog, who was coming down the track towards them again, presumably on the homeward stretch of their walk. The dog—a very cute miniature schnauzer—ran towards them and the woman called it back with an apologetic smile.

'I doubt there's enough time anyway.' There was a wicked edge to Aiden's smile as the woman disappeared along the track. 'It'll get cold around here when the sun goes down.'

He wanted a whole night with her? The thought made Sophia's toes curl. But this was a daytime date.

Oh, help… What if there was a rule about not going any further until date number three? What if this three-dates business was just a build-up for a one-night stand?

Hard not to believe that it would be worth waiting for, if that was the case.

'We have options,' Aiden added. 'You get to choose.'

'Oh?' Maybe one of those options included going somewhere really private. Sophia grinned. 'Fire away. I like choosing.'

'Option one: we could take the ferry over to Sorrento to get dessert. There's a shop there that has the best vanilla slices in the world and we might get to see some dolphins on the way.'

Sophia nodded thoughtfully. He really had planned

this date carefully. Or—the thought sent a chill down her spine—was this a standard number-two date?

'Option two is a swim. The water is probably arctic but it's warm enough to dry off on the beach and, by then, it'll be about time to head home.'

Home? To his place? After getting almost naked and lying in the sun for a while? It wasn't hard to make a choice.

'It would be a shame to come to the seaside and not have a swim.'

'I knew you were brave.' The kiss was swift but sweet. 'Let's go.'

The walk made the day seem even warmer and by the time they went down the sandy stairs to the endless white beach with a misty lighthouse far away, they were more than ready to pull off their clothes and brave the curl of the surf. The beach was a popular place to be but most people were sunbathing. Some sat in beach chairs, reading, and others were having picnics or playing ball games. There were children paddling and building sand-castles but there were very few people swimming.

And no wonder. The first splash of water was cold enough to make Sophia shriek but Aiden simply laughed and dived through the next wave. She jumped up and down as she went further out, getting more of her body wet each time, and suddenly it wasn't so bad. And then Aiden surfaced right beside her and his smile made her aware of the silky caress of the sea water over her entire body.

'This is gorgeous,' she called over the sound of the waves. 'I love it.'

'I knew you would,' he called back. 'You're my kind of girl.'

They couldn't stay in the water for long and they were both shivering as they towelled themselves dry but then they lay on their towels on the soft sand and there was enough warmth in the sun for the chill to ebb slowly away.

For the longest time, they lay there, absorbing the warmth. Side by side on their backs, saying nothing. And then Sophia felt the brush of Aiden's fingers and his hand curl itself around hers.

'I really like you, Sophia.'

'I really like you, too, Aiden.' Sophia's eyes were still closed and her smile grew slowly. She couldn't remember the last time she'd felt this happy. Even the noises around them—the roll of the waves and the shouting of children enjoying themselves—only added to this feeling of contentment. 'I think this has been the best second date I've ever been on.'

Aiden tightened his grip on Sophia's hand. This was by far the best second date he'd ever been on as well. The only thing wrong with it was that it would have to end soon. They were almost dry and they needed to get dressed again because the heat of the day would start dropping rapidly before long. They had a long ride to get back to the city as well and by then it would be evening. They both had an early start for work tomorrow but did that really mean that it had to be over? Sophia believed that he'd planned this whole date after they'd agreed to go to a beach. She didn't need to know that he'd kept his options open and hadn't planned it to continue on into the evening, did she?

'It's not over yet.'

He heard the words come out of his mouth and they felt...right. Of course it couldn't be over yet.

'Oh? What else is in the plan?'

He could hear the smile in Sophia's voice. And something more. A willingness to go along with whatever he wanted?

He wanted to take Sophia home. To his bed. Okay, they both needed to get to work early but there were a lot of hours between now and then. Why shouldn't they make the most of every single one of them?

'Well, I was thinking...' Aiden propped himself up on one elbow. Maybe he didn't need to say anything here. He could just kiss her again. And then he could look into her eyes and he'd know whether she was happy with the new plan.

He let his mouth hover over hers for a deliciously long moment. Feeling the tingle of their lips not quite touching. Knowing just how much better it was going to get in a nanosecond.

And then he heard it. Faintly at first but getting steadily louder.

Sophia's lips moved under his. Tickling. 'What *is* that?'

'My phone.' He didn't want to answer it. Dammit... all he wanted to do was kiss Sophia but her lips were moving again. Smiling?

'It's a *siren*?'

'Yeah, I know. Cheesy. My kid brother chose it for me.'

And it could be that kid brother who was calling right now. Highly likely to be, seeing as they hadn't spoken yet today. In fact, they hadn't spoken very often for a few days now. Ever since that tense conversation about Aiden smothering Nate because of his misplaced guilt.

He still wanted to kiss Sophia more than answer it but something else was making his skin prickle and he recognised that sensation.

Guilt. He barely knew this woman and suddenly she was more important than his brother? What was he thinking?

'I'd better get that. Sorry.'

'No problem.'

A soft breeze had sprung up, making it colder. Or maybe he just had more skin exposed as he sat up and rummaged in his coat pocket for his phone. Sure enough, the caller ID said 'Nate'. Aiden swiped the screen.

'Hey... What's up?'

'Guess.'

'I can't. You'll have to tell me.'

'I went for the team trials today.'

'Yeah? How'd that go?'

'I got in, man. I'm in the team.'

'That's...fantastic.' The smile that pulled at his lips was genuine. 'Great news. I reckon it calls for a cele-bration.'

'Too right. We're having a few beers back at our place. Thought you might want to drop by.'

He was listening to Nate but he was looking at Sophia. She still lay on her back, shading her eyes from the sun with her arm. Her hair was still damp and looked almost black where it lay against the pale skin of her shoulders. He couldn't help his gaze travelling further. Over the rest of that gorgeous, soft-looking skin and the perfect proportions of her small, slim body.

He'd never wanted anybody this much.

He'd have to take a rain-check on that celebratory beer with Nate because otherwise he wouldn't get to take Sophia home and make love to her properly.

Slowly...

Or maybe not so slowly the first time...

His throat suddenly felt dry.

'You still there, man? Where *are* you, anyway?'

Impressions flashed through Aiden's brain with the speed of light. That note in Nate's voice when he'd made that suggestion so casually that he 'might' want to drop by.

Things hadn't been quite right between them since that conversation the other day. And if he didn't join in the celebration of Nate making the Murderball team, it could be interpreted as not being supportive of his brother as he achieved one of his long-held ambitions and that could push them further apart. What then? Would Nate choose not to even tell him when he was moving out of the house to try living independently?

His brother was trying out his wings and surely that meant that now—more than ever—he needed support. Aiden had to be there for him one hundred per cent.

How could he even entertain the idea of letting a woman get between them? It wasn't as if she'd still be in his life in a week or two from now but Nate would be. He would always be in his life and he'd always take priority.

'I'm still here,' he said. 'Bad line. I'm out of the city but I'll be back soon.'

'No worries. You went for a ride? You on a date or something?'

'Yeah...Queenscliff.'

'Oh...of course. This is your number two with Sophia. Hey...hope I'm not interrupting anything.' His laugh made a lie of his words but didn't quite ring true for some reason.

'Not at all. Just went for swim, would you believe?'

'Well, don't hurry back, man. Enjoy yourself. Catch you soon.'

The beeping signalled that Nate had hung up. The note of disappointment in his words was still there, though. And the odd edge to the laughter as he'd tried to make light of things.

Aiden dragged his eyes away from Sophia. Closed them, in fact.

'Not a problem,' he heard himself saying into the silence of a dead line. At least he could sound reluctant now. As though there was something he really had to do even though he didn't want to. 'I'll get there as soon as I can.'

Sophia was already pulling her clothes on by the time he shoved his phone back into his pocket.

'Sorry about that.'

'It's not a problem.' He could hear the note of determined cheerfulness in her voice as she echoed his own words. 'We've had a lovely day. If there's somewhere else you need to be now, it's okay. I understand.'

She might understand but he could see the disappointment in her eyes and he felt like a jerk. He could say it wasn't that important and the only place he needed to be for now was with her.

But Nate was disappointed too. He'd have that in the back of his mind all evening if he stayed with Sophia.

The feeling of being torn was unpleasant. The desire to tell Sophia he only wanted to be with her was strong enough to ring warning bells.

It wasn't supposed to feel like this. It was supposed to be fun.

For both of them.

And it wasn't any more, was it? How could being between a rock and a hard place ever be considered fun?

He pulled his clothes on, feeling the added unpleasantness of the sand in his shoes. He watched Sophia roll up her damp towel and shove it in her beach bag.

'You dry enough? It'll be cold on the bike, otherwise.'

'I'm fine. I've got my coat.'

The coat wasn't enough to make her feel fine.

Not at all.

Maybe it would have helped if they'd been able to talk but there was no way they could do that on a bike. Sophia held onto Aiden's waist and kept her face hidden against his back. Damp tendrils of hair still flicked her face and her skin was cold enough to make them sting.

How had that happened?

One minute she'd been feeling more blissful than she could remember ever feeling and then it had all gone wrong, the atmosphere lost thanks to the intrusion of a phone call. He'd just been about to kiss her. To tell her the plans that meant the date wasn't over yet.

Why hadn't he just ignored the call? Why did he have a stupid siren call tone that made it impossible for anyone to ignore? Just as impossible as it was not to think it was probably another woman who'd been calling him. Was he already lining up the next contender in his three-dates game?

What was so fantastic about the news he'd received? Was whoever she was available? *Tonight?*

It wasn't fair. Their first date hadn't really counted and date number two had just been sabotaged.

So much for getting out there and having some fun.

This wasn't fun at all any more.

Did she even want a third—and last—date?

There was plenty of time on that long, cold ride to turn that question over in her head. As she made her stiff limbs co-operate in climbing off the big, red bike in front of her house and her fingers work well enough to undo her helmet and hand it back, Sophia was sure that this was goodbye and she had decided that she was quite happy about that.

She was, in fact, more angry than disappointed now.

But then Aiden caught her gaze and held it.

'I'm really sorry about this,' he said. 'If I could get out of it, I would.'

There was something in his gaze that told her he was being absolutely sincere. That he wanted to be with her—maybe even more than she'd wanted him to be. And that it *was* something really important that was dragging him away.

She wanted to tell him that it didn't matter. That they still had one date left so everything would be okay. That it was no big deal.

But the words wouldn't come out. She managed half a smile. A shrug that said, Yeah, it sucks but that's life, isn't it?

And then she turned away and went into her house without a backward glance, leaning her forehead against the closed door until she heard the sound of a motorbike's engine being gunned and then fading into silence.

'What are you doing here?'

Aiden held up the six-pack of beer. 'I heard there was a bit of a celebration going on.'

Nate had been the one who'd come to open the door when Aiden had rung the bell. The wide hallway of the old house was empty behind him.

'You ditched your date to come *here*?'

Aiden's shrug said that it was no big deal but Nate shook his head and his huff of sound was disgusted. 'Man, you're an idiot. How d'you think that made Sophia feel?'

The cardboard handle of the beer pack was cutting into Aiden's hand. He had been an idiot. He'd made Sophia feel bad only to find he wasn't welcome here.

Something was going wrong in his life right now. The wheels were still turning but it felt like they weren't quite on the tracks and he couldn't, for the life of him, figure out why. He looked away from Nate.

'I thought this was more important.' He cleared his throat. 'And…I wanted to…I dunno…put things right,

I guess. Wouldn't want you to think I don't support you in whatever you want to do.'

Nate gave an audible snort this time. 'It's only selection. Miss my first game next week and you'll definitely be in trouble.'

The lightness in his tone didn't match the expression on his face when Aiden turned back. Nate understood what he'd been too clumsy to articulate well and held up his hand, the fingers curled into a fist. 'There's nothing to put right, man. We're brothers. Family.'

Aiden bumped the fist with his own. Nate shook his head but he was grinning as he swivelled the chair on the polished floor. 'Seeing as you're here, you might as well come in for a beer. Hey, what do you call a quadriplegic in a pile of leaves?'

There was relief to be found as he followed Nate towards the lounge. Enough to stop the automatic protest at a joke that would seem so distasteful to people outside this community.

'I dunno. What?'

'Russell.'

There was even more relief in the shared laughter but it still wasn't quite enough to put the wheels completely back on track. Nate had said there was nothing to put right but that wasn't entirely true, was it?

Things had gone unexpectedly wrong with someone else as well. A woman he'd had no desire at all to hurt. Quite the opposite, in fact.

How on earth was he going to put that right?

CHAPTER SIX

'YOU OKAY?'

'A bit nervous, I think. I watched a Caesarean before but I've never been actually involved.'

'I won't ask you to do anything you're not ready to cope with, don't worry.'

Flick nodded, pulling her theatre cap over her dark blonde hair. She looked a bit pale, Sophia thought, which was probably nerves on top of the weariness of a long day.

She was feeling weary herself. It didn't help that she'd been feeling as flat as a pancake ever since that date with Aiden had ended on such an unsatisfactory note.

She hadn't heard from him since and the mix of disappointment and—it had to be admitted—frustration had made her wonder if the downside of dating outweighed any of the potential benefits.

She'd brushed off Flick's friendly query about how the date had gone and she'd tried really hard to focus on her work and let the satisfaction her job always gave her chase the blues away, but that hadn't worked very well today either. Not when they were now in a situation none of them had expected—or wanted—to be in.

They should be heading home by now, after the home birth of their patient Kim's second baby, but things hadn't gone according to plan and, after transferring Kim to the MMU hours ago, a Caesarean section had been deemed the best option for an exhausted mother and a now distressed baby.

Kim and her husband, Peter, were in the theatre's anteroom under the care of an anaesthetist as she received an epidural.

'Put some theatre booties on over your shoes.' Sophia pulled the disposable covers from the dispenser on the wall of the changing room. 'And here's a mask.'

'Do we have to scrub in as well?'

'No. We don't go anywhere near the operating site. Our role is to support Kim in getting the best birth experience she can under the circumstances.'

'Like making sure she gets the skin-to-skin contact?'

'Exactly. But only if the baby's well enough, of course. We have to be prepared, though. What's the most important thing to make sure we've sorted?'

'That her gown can be moved without disturbing the theatre drapes?'

'Good.' Sophia smiled at her student. 'Now, let's get moving. We've got a few things to organise. I'm going to liaise with the ward and check that a midwife is available to take transfer of care in the recovery room and I want you to ring the lab and order a bucket of iced water.'

'For the cord blood gas samples?'

'You're onto it. We've also got to check that both the

transport cot and the resuscitation cot are turned on and I want to make sure you know where all the equipment is. Follow me.'

There was a hum of activity in Theatre as the staff prepared for the surgery.

'We'll move the resuscitation cot over to here,' Sophia decided.

'Why?'

'Hopefully, it's not going to be needed, but if it is, we want a line of direct vision for both the parents so they can maintain visual contact with their baby at all times.'

Kim was wheeled in moments later. Lights were shifted and positioned and monitoring equipment attached. An ECG trace blipped into action on an overhead screen and numbers flashed and changed as they displayed heart rate, blood pressure and blood oxygen levels. Sophia showed Peter where he was allowed to stand, checked the function of the foetal monitor and then smiled at Kim.

'All good?'

'I'm scared.'

'I know.' Sophia squeezed her patient's hand, careful not to dislodge the IV line. 'You've got a fantastic team who are here to look after you and you'll be amazed how fast it goes.'

'I'm not sure any more...about...you know...'

'Watching baby come out?' Sophia glanced at the drape screen the theatre nurses were putting up at chest level. The plan had been to lower the screen after the incision to the uterus had been made but another glance showed how pale Peter was looking. A definite contender for fainting.

'You don't have to see that bit,' she told Kim. 'We can still put baby straight onto your chest.' Her gaze caught Flick's. 'Let's put a chair in for Peter. That way he can hold Kim's hand and he doesn't have to see anything he doesn't want to either.'

The surgeon and her registrar came into Theatre and, for a while at least, Sophia could totally forget about her personal life as she got caught up in one of the more dramatic ways to bring a new life into the world.

She made sure Flick could stand close enough to see what was happening as the surgeon and her registrar stood on either side of Kim's swollen abdomen. The only sounds were the beeping of the monitors and the calm requests for instruments as the initial incision was made and then the tissues quickly dissected with gloved fingers in use more often than a scalpel or scissors.

Sophia was sure that Flick was holding her breath— as she always did—when the careful incision into the uterus was made and they could see the dark whorls of wet hair on the baby's head. Forceps were fitted to lift the head far enough for the surgeon to be able to hold it with her hands and then the baby was eased out, pausing long enough for the registrar to suction the infant's airways.

The baby's eyes were open and an arm waving slowly. Sophia breathed a sigh of relief. It started crying as its legs were lifted clear of the uterus and she heard a gasp that was more like a strangled sob of relief from both Peter and Kim. Flick was focused on the registrar clamping and cutting the cord but then her gaze caught Sophia's and she gave a quick nod. She took the baby from the registrar as Flick helped a nurse to move the screen and she could place the newborn on her mother's chest.

The longest part of the surgery came now, with the precise task of repairing all the layers of tissue, but, with the screen back in place, Kim was unaware of what was happening and time ceased to matter as she and Peter touched and marvelled at their new baby.

'Did you note the time and sex of the baby?'

Flick nodded. 'I've got the labels ready for the cord blood gas samples.'

'Good. Now, double-check this with me. We have to make sure that the details on the maternal and neonatal wrist labels match.'

Thirty minutes later, Kim was ready to be transferred to a ward bed and taken into Recovery. The paediatrician had checked their daughter and she was wrapped and warm. Sophia put the small bundle into Peter's arms to be carried into Recovery. The transfer of care to the ward midwife would happen there but Sophia wasn't ready to leave yet. This was her favourite time after the tension of a Caesarean, to help with the first breastfeed and watch the bonding happening between the baby and her parents. Kim's mother was waiting nearby, too, with their three-year-old son, who would be able to come and meet his new sister before they got transferred to the ward.

'That was amazing,' Flick said quietly, when they were finally heading home. 'But I am *so* tired.' She stepped into the lift and leaned against the wall.

'Me too. This is when you really feel it, when the excitement's all over.' Sophia pushed the button to take them to the ground floor. It wasn't just physical weariness either. With the prospect of heading home alone as soon as she stepped out of the Victoria's front doors, she knew that she would end up feeling flatter than ever. 'The café will still be open. Let's go and get a coffee.'

Flick groaned. 'Oh, no...not coffee. Even the thought of it makes me feel ill.'

'Really?' Sophia's head swivelled to take a closer look at her student. 'That's not like you.' She noted the pale skin and dark circles under Flick's eyes. Something clicked into place. 'Wait...you're not pregnant, are you?'

'I think it's just something I ate.'

The lift stopped with a jerk as she spoke and then the doors slid open but was that enough to explain the way Flick was avoiding her gaze?

'I've got to go. See you tomorrow, Soph.'

'Hang on...' She'd put her foot in it, even making the suggestion, hadn't she? It certainly hadn't been her intention to upset her student. 'Hey...I'm sorry, Flick. I didn't—'

Flick raised her hand, without turning. 'It's okay. I'm fine. Really.'

'Sophia?'

The voice from behind made her spin round without thinking. It was so unexpected. So...welcome?

'Aiden... What are you doing here?'

No. It wasn't welcome. She didn't want to talk to him right now. She needed to talk to Flick. Or maybe Flick needed to talk to *her*. Turning her head again, just as quickly, she could see Flick disappearing towards the front doors. She could hardly run away from Aiden.

She didn't want to talk to him. He'd interrupted a conversation she'd been having with her student and she was on the brink of excusing herself and running away.

He didn't want that to happen. Catching sight of her as she'd stepped out of the lift had been like a slap in the face. Enough to bring back the guilt he'd been wrestling with ever since he'd cut their date short to go and see Nathan.

He'd picked up the phone half a dozen times since then, with the intention of trying to contact Sophia, but something had always got in the way. A call to a job made it easy to hang up but it was never enough of an excuse. He'd been...scared? Well, nervous anyway. He hadn't been able to come up with any plausible plan to put things right so he'd known he could well make things worse. And he hadn't wanted to face the potential rejection.

But actually seeing her instead of a faceless phone call brought back all the reasons why he wanted to put things right.

She looked tired. The way she stared after her student had a worried edge to it. And he could sense that her mood was different. More serious. Sad, even? Oh, help...was he flattering himself or could that have something to do with him?

Despite all of that—or maybe because of it—she was still the most gorgeous woman he'd ever met. He wanted to put his arms around her and hold her close. Kiss whatever it was better. But he could only say something and hope that she might choose to stay in his company for just a little longer. Long enough for him to think of something. Some way to put things right.

'I came in to check up on a patient from today,' he heard himself saying. 'Cyclist that got clipped by a tram. I was worried about her.'

'Oh...' A rush of mixed emotions washed through Sophia. The attraction that came from imagining him on the job, weaving through heavy traffic with the lights and siren going on that huge bike. Admiration that came from knowing how calmly he would have taken charge of the emergency. Warmth that came from knowing that he did care about his patients.

And there was more threaded through those feelings. She couldn't pretend that the personal attraction had been quashed by the disappointment of that last date. Maybe the strongest memory right now was the sincerity she'd seen in his eyes when he'd left her on the footpath. She'd been too angry to believe that he wouldn't have been abandoning her unless it had been for something too important to ignore, but that anger had faded into the flatness of the last few days.

She wanted to believe it now.

She wanted...

'Would you like to grab a coffee or something?' Aiden seemed to be watching her carefully, as though he was aware of the struggle she was having, trying to capture a thought that would determine her response to this unexpected meeting.

'I...um...' There was no point looking towards the

main entrance but she turned her head again anyway, despite knowing that Flick was long gone.

'Do you need to catch up with her?'

'No.' Sophia pushed her concern about her student to one side. She would see her soon enough and, if that startling suspicion had any grounds, it would only become more apparent with the passing of time. She sucked in a breath and looked back at Aiden.

'I was planning to get a coffee,' she admitted. 'It's been a long day. We had a case that got complicated and we had to bring her in for a Caesarean. And...' Something she couldn't identify was melting away deep inside her. 'I believe I still owe you a coffee?'

Aiden's smile lit up his face and she saw a flash of what looked like relief in his eyes.

'I believe you do.'

The tension eased as they began walking towards the cafeteria together but now Sophia was aware of how she must look. Her hair had been squashed beneath a cap for too long and she had crumpled scrubs on under her jacket. Any make-up she'd started the day with must have worn off long ago and she was probably tired enough to look years older.

Except that—oddly—she didn't feel that tired any more. And a sideways glance showed that Aiden's uniform was pretty crumpled as well. His boots looked scuffed and he had a big scratch on one hand.

For both of them, their appearance was nothing more than evidence of what they did for a living. A badge of honour even?

Aiden held the door of the cafeteria open for Sophia.

The relief he'd felt when she'd agreed to have a coffee with him should have been a warning but he was going to ignore it. So what if it felt like a major victory? That the wheels were back on exactly the right tracks? It shouldn't feel this good, of course. Not when all he might be winning was the chance for a third—and final—date.

But he was feeling better than he had for days so why shouldn't he make the most of it? Sophia looked happier too. She was smiling as they headed for the machine that provided coffee that was dreadful but free. She put a polystyrene cup under the dispenser.

'What can I get you?' she asked. 'Cappuccino? A latte?'

'I think a long black might be the safest choice.'

'Done.' With the button pushed the machine whirred into life. 'And I think I might push the boat out and have a hot chocolate.'

There would be a rush before too long, when staff on an early dinner break came in, but, for now, the cafeteria was almost completely deserted. They found a table in the corner and sat down. Sophia was at right angles to Aiden. Their knees bumped under the table and the eye contact they made was instantaneous. And intense enough to make her heart skip a beat.

'This doesn't count as a date,' she murmured.

'Of course not.' Aiden nodded, his face serious. 'It wasn't planned so how could it be?'

'Mmm.'

'And besides...we never got to finish date number two, did we?'

'Ah...' The tension was back again. They had to both

be thinking of that moment. Not that any words had been spoken but Sophia could actually feel the impression of that half-smile she'd summoned. The dismissive way she'd shrugged and turned away. 'No...' She had to drop her gaze. 'It didn't feel finished.'

'We should do something about that, then.'

It took courage to meet his gaze. 'Yes. I think maybe we should.'

The intensity humming between them bore no relation to the casual words from Aiden.

'I've got a thing I have to go to tomorrow night. Would you like to come with me?'

'What sort of a thing?'

Not that it mattered. She would have agreed to go anywhere with him.

Or maybe it did matter. A flicker of something in Aiden's face made Sophia realise that, whatever it was, it was important to him. That he was inviting her into a part of his life that might not be something he shared with just anyone. That he was taking a risk?

'A surprise,' he said, after that tiny hesitation. 'If I tell you what it is, that would make it more like a new date and it's not. It's—'

'A half-date?' Sophia suggested.

'Just a thing. Let's not try and define it.'

'Okay.'

'So you'll come?'

'Sure. How could I resist? I've never been to a "thing" before. I'm intrigued.'

'Don't get too excited. It's a bit...different.'

'I'm even more intrigued now. Give me a clue?'

'Uh-uh.' Aiden shook his head but he was smiling. 'I'll pick you up at seven-thirty.'

'Dress code?'

'Definitely casual. And warm.' Aiden took a sip of his coffee and made a face. 'This is awful. I don't even think it deserves to be called coffee.'

A bubble of happiness made Sophia giggle. 'Guess I still owe you one, then.'

Aiden's nod was thoughtful. 'I'll put this in the category of medication. Something to wake me up after a tough day.'

'So what happened? How badly injured was your cyclist?'

'Multi-trauma. She's up in Intensive Care now but I wanted to see what had been found. The head injury made her combative so it was hard to assess her.'

Sophia nodded. She had plenty of questions and was genuinely interested in the responses as Aiden told her more about the case, but there was an undercurrent that made it all so much more enjoyable.

She was going to see him again tomorrow night.

They were going to a *thing*...

Parking outside a suburban gymnasium was a surprise. So the 'thing' was a sporting event of some kind? This was weird but Sophia was prepared to keep an open mind, especially when Aiden took her hand to lead her inside.

And there was another surprise. The seats were crowded and the atmosphere loud and vibrant but the last thing she'd expected to see were the teams on the basketball-style court. They were all young men and they were all in wheelchairs.

'What is this?'

'Murderball.' Aiden waved to a girl with spiky black hair and facial piercings who was in the first row of seats. 'Wheelchair rugby.' He led her towards some empty seats in the third row. 'It's my brother's first game.'

Wow. No wonder she'd got the impression that this was a private part of Aiden's life.

'Your brother is paraplegic?'

'Tetraplegic. You have to have disability in all four limbs to qualify to play.'

'But...' Sophia stared at the activity below as she took her seat. The team members were rolling across the floor with some doing fast spins, looking like they were warming up. They were definitely using their hands and arms.

'There's a scale,' Aiden told her. 'The level of disability is graded from zero point five, which is the greatest restriction, to three point five. If you were able-bodied you'd score five and if you were totally paralysed you'd be a zero. There are four on the court at any one time and they have to have a total score between them of no more than eight points.'

The teams were lining up, face to face in the centre of the court, and then they peeled off, high-fiving each other.

'Which one is your brother?'

'Number three for the Melbourne Mobsters. The red and black team. He's not going to be on in the first quarter. He may not get on at all but I hope he does. This is his first game.'

'Oh...' That made it even more of a big deal to be here. No wonder Aiden was looking tense, with his jaw knotted and his focus intently on the court. Sophia slipped her hand over his to give it a squeeze and found it caught and gripped hard.

'What's his name?' Sophia grinned. 'Just so I can yell when he scores a goal.'

'Nathan. Nate.'

A whistle blew and the referee threw a ball high in the air and then it was all on. A player for the Canberra Cowboys put the ball on his lap and sped away from the others to cross the goal line between cones. A cheer erupted from the crowd but it was nothing on the noise level when one of the local boys scored less than a minute later.

The game was fast and furious and Sophia was hooked well before the first quarter ended. She gasped at the first collision she saw between three players going for the ball that made the chairs tip and her jaw dropped when one player fell backwards with a crash, but the game carried on with a supporter rushing onto the court to right the upturned chair, and within seconds the fall was forgotten.

A hooter sounded to signal the rolling rotation of the players but Nathan wasn't one of the new team members. Sophia tried to figure out the rules but the game was so fast, she was having trouble. This was like a mix of basketball, rugby and bumper cars.

'Why do they bounce the ball sometimes?'

'You have to either bounce it or pass it to someone else within ten seconds.'

'What happened there?'

'Penalty awarded for a foul. That cowboy hit a mobster's chair behind the main axle, which makes it spin out of control.'

Scores jumped quickly but stayed close. The noise level steadily increased until Sophia had to shout to be heard as the final quarter began.

'That's Nathan. He's *on*.'

She'd barely known this game existed before coming here tonight, but suddenly it felt personal. Nathan looked a lot younger than Aiden and he looked a bit nervous. Sophia felt nervous herself. The chairs were clearly designed to cope with the impacts with their metal bumpers and spoke guards. And the players wore gloves and elbow protection but surely there was a huge potential for injury down there?

Aiden obviously thought so too, given the way he winced visibly the first time Nathan's chair got hit. But, moments later, a wide overhead pass from the other side of the court saw Nathan catch the ball and dump it on his lap. He spun his chair on the spot and took off, his arms almost a blur as he powered towards the goal line. Three other chairs converged on his path but he saw them as he looked up to bounce the ball off to one side. With another lightning-fast spin, he changed direction and had a clear line to speed towards the cones.

The cheer was the loudest yet. Maybe because she and Aiden were both on their feet, yelling at the tops of their voices. She saw the girl in the front row, who'd waved at Aiden when they arrived, leaping about and waving two huge pompoms in the red and black team colours.

The Melbourne Mobsters lost by two points but it didn't seem to matter. The crowd was happy to cheer any of the players who came close enough to the spectators to receive a high five or a kiss from a girlfriend. Still holding Sophia's hand, Aiden pulled her towards the front row as a chair rolled directly towards them. Nathan got a kiss from the girl with the spiky black hair and then a fist bump and a one-armed hug from his brother.

'You made it. Didn't see you up there, bro.'

'Wouldn't have missed it for the world. You rocked it, man.'

Sophia nodded her agreement, unable to wipe the grin off her face. 'Most exciting game I've ever watched,' she said. 'Of anything.'

Nathan Harrison's eyes were the same unusual shade of brown as Aiden's and they had the same ability to focus with instant intensity. The slow grin was eerily familiar as well.

'You have to be Sophia,' he said.

She nodded again but didn't miss the glance that flicked between the brothers. Or the disconcerting way Nathan was shaking his head as he looked back, still grinning.

He must have seen her confusion. 'Sorry. It's just that it's the first time I've met one of Aiden's girlfriends. He doesn't usually give me the honour.'

Because a three-dates rule didn't allow for inclusion in a private part of his life? She hadn't imagined that hesitation in inviting her, had she? Or underplayed the

significance? But she had no idea whether it meant anything. Or whether she even wanted it to mean anything.

The moment could have been incredibly awkward but
it was the girl beside Nathan who saved it.

'There's a first time for everything,' she declared.
'Otherwise nothing would ever change.' She grinned at
Sophia. 'I'm Sam,' she said. 'And I'm delighted to meet
you—which is what Nate's really trying to say.'

'I knew that.' It was impossible to miss the significance in the glance Sam shared with Nathan. Their love
for each other was blindingly obvious.

So was the bond between the brothers. Aiden de-
clined the invitation to join the team and supporters at
a local bar, saying he had a horribly early start the next
day, but she could hear the fierce pride in his voice when
they took their leave.

'You did good, man. Can't wait for the next game.'

Aiden could feel the remnants of a ridiculously proud
smile he'd been suppressing as he started up the old van
he'd used to collect Sophia that evening. He could also
feel the way she was looking at him. The intensity was
almost palpable.

'Aiden?'

'Yeah?'

'That call you got at the beach the other day.'

'Yeah?' Oh, help. He'd hoped that had been forgotten
by now. That he'd put things right. It had needed something special and inviting her into a part of his life he'd
never shared with a woman had seemed like the way to
go, but maybe he'd been wrong.

Maybe he was still in the dog box.

'Was it a call from Nathan?'

'Um…yeah…' He turned his head, the query of why she was asking on the tip of his tongue but the word never escaped.

He didn't need to ask why.

She understood.

She might not have any idea why the bond was so strong between him and Nathan but she knew it was there and how important it was.

Weirdly, he could feel something inside his chest crack and something warm seeped out.

Something really nice.

He did have a really early start tomorrow but that hadn't been the real reason for declining the after-game social occasion with the team. He'd known he wanted to take Sophia home and be alone with her.

And the desire to do that had just leapt right off the scale.

CHAPTER SEVEN

THIS WAS THE way the last date should have ended.

Once again, Sophia was pressed against her front door the moment it shut behind her but she wasn't standing there with her head bowed, listening to the sound of a fading engine.

This time, it was her back against the door. And her arms, as she lifted them in a helpless gesture, unable to think of anything else to do with them as she met the intensity of the kiss she was receiving.

Who knew that you could actually *taste* desire? Was it her own or Aiden's or the chemical reaction of mixing them that made this so incredibly delicious?

For the longest time, that was enough. The silky glide of tongue against tongue. The endless variations of pressure in lips that was a conversation all by itself. But then Aiden's hands left her neck, where they'd been cradling her head, and they trailed down to cup her breasts. His lips left hers to touch the soft skin below her ear where she could feel her own pulse pounding and suddenly it wasn't enough.

Not nearly enough.

And she knew what to do with her arms, now, too. She could wrap them around his neck and run her fingers through the softness of that closely cropped hair. Press her lips against that vulnerable spot on his temple.

She couldn't say who started moving first. If it hadn't been her, Aiden didn't seem to have any problem finding her bedroom, but it was a tiny house. The interruption of removing clothes felt like a nuisance and Sophia hastily stripped off her sweater at the same time Aiden peeled off his leather jacket. They both kicked off their shoes but then they looked at each other and abandoned undressing to kiss again.

And time seemed to stop. Taking their clothes off was no longer a nuisance. It was a game to be savoured. A slow reveal of buttons coming undone and zips being separated. Exposed skin that needed exploring. Touching and kissing with murmurs of appreciation and the odd whimper of escalating desire.

Too soon—and not nearly soon enough—they were in her bed and now there were no limits on the touching. No stopping the roller-coaster of sensation that was pushing them towards ecstasy. The interruption of Aiden leaning over the side of the bed to find his discarded jeans and fish in the pocket for a foil packet was unbearable.

There's no need, Sophia wanted to say. *Don't stop.*

But, of course, she didn't say it. And it wasn't entirely true, anyway. Okay, there was no way she could get pregnant but there were other reasons to use protection...

And maybe that was why she found the interruption unbearable. She didn't want to have to think about anything like that—even for the few seconds it took.

Easy to forget about it again, though. To cry out with the pleasure of feeling him inside her and then to simply surrender to the mounting tension that was taking them both to that place like no other. Where the world could stop turning for as long as it took.

It took quite a while for either of them to get their breath back as they lay there, their limbs entangled and the only sound their rapid panting.

'Oh, my God,' Sophia whispered, when words were finally available. 'How did you *do* that?'

'I was going to ask you the same thing.' There was a smile in Aiden's voice as he eased himself free. He didn't let go of Sophia, though, and she found herself rolling onto to her side, with her head cradled against his chest. 'You're amazing. You do know that, don't you?'

She could feel the edge of his nipple against her lips as she smiled. 'I do now. You're pretty amazing yourself.'

He pressed his lips to the top of her head. 'Maybe it was the combination.'

'Mmm.' Post-coital drowsiness was enveloping Sophia. She could feel herself relaxing into sleep and the thought that she would wake in Aiden's arms was blissful.

But he moved, just a little. 'I should go,' he murmured. 'I wasn't kidding about the early start.'

'You don't have to.'

The soft sound was regretful. 'But I know exactly what would happen if I stayed and I only had one condom in my pocket.'

The temptation to say something was even stronger this time. 'You don't need to worry about me getting pregnant.'

He moved enough to break the contact between their bodies. 'Don't take it personally but I've never relied on anyone else for contraception and I'm not about to break that rule.'

'Oh…' Sophia could feel the chill of exposed skin. And then she felt the dip of her mattress as Aiden sat up and swung his legs over the side of the bed.

He turned then but it was too dark to read his expression. 'I'm never going to have kids,' he said quietly. 'I had to be a father to Nate when he was growing up and that was enough. More than enough.'

There was a world of pain behind those words. But there was also a warning note. He'd shared more than his body with her tonight. He'd shared a lot of his personal life but there were limits. This wasn't something he was ready to talk about.

He leaned towards her and gave her a swift kiss. 'I do have to go.'

'Okay.'

Sophia listened to the sounds of him getting dressed again. She sat up, pulling the duvet around her like a shawl.

'It was the best half-date I've ever been on,' she told him. 'Thank you.'

The glimmer of his smile gave her the impression she'd said exactly the right thing. Not pushing him to talk any more about his 'rules' or the reason they were so iron-clad.

He came close and this time the kiss lingered.

'Just as well it was a half-date,' he said. 'That means we still have one left.'

One.

Sophia's heart sank.

'Would it count as a date if we didn't go anywhere? Like—if you came round for dinner one night or something?'

Something like a chuckle rumbled in Aiden's chest. 'I don't reckon it would. Do you?'

'No.' Sophia injected complete authority into her voice. 'I'm quite sure it wouldn't. Give me your phone number and I'll text you when I've had time to go shopping.'

Finding time to go grocery shopping wasn't so hard because there were supermarkets that regularly stayed open until at least midnight.

Finding time to cook something as amazing as Sophia wanted it to be was another matter. With what felt like a blinding flash of inspiration, a couple of days later she remembered the slow cooker tucked away at the back of one of her kitchen cupboards. Perfect. Getting up a little earlier to get ready for work, she had time to sear meat and brown the vegetables and then all she had to do was push the button and let the cooker work its magic while she worked with Flick for another busy day of home visits.

The concern about her student was still there but had been pushed into the background. Flick had dismissed her reaction to coffee after that Caesarean case as being due to a bit of a tummy bug and Sophia had

been embarrassed that she'd blurted out the first suspicion that had sprung to mind—that Flick might be
pregnant. The fact that she'd been pale and quiet for a
few days after that fitted with her having been off colour and if she still seemed on the quiet side now, that
could well be due to the extra studying she was doing.
Flick seemed determined to learn everything about her
chosen career and today was a great one for introduc-
ing her to things she hadn't done before.

It was good for her to have her teaching to distract
her, as well. If she hadn't had Flick in the car with her
as she negotiated the heavy traffic in places, she might
have been tempted to wonder about how that meal was
progressing as it simmered gently.

Or notice the desire that was simmering a little less
gently deep in her belly. Would they go to bed again?
Or maybe the real question was when and not if. Before
or after dinner?

The car jerked a little with the firm pressure of her
foot on the accelerator. 'What do you think is the most
important thing about the postnatal care we give for up
to six weeks after birth?'

'Support,' Flick answered promptly. 'Help with things
like breastfeeding and bathing baby and how to cope
with fatigue.'

'And?'

'Monitoring the health of both the baby and the
mother. Especially after a Caesarean in case of infection. And making sure they don't think that breastfeeding is a reliable form of contraception.'

Hmm. Expanding on that topic was not going to help her stay focused. 'Good. What else do we do?'

'Watch out for signs of postnatal depression?'

They discussed the kind of signs that could be important as Sophia drove them to their first visit of the day but their first mother—Judith—seemed to be coping extremely well, having had a home birth two days ago.

'I'm lucky I've got Mum staying. I'm getting plenty of sleep between feeds.'

'Looks like baby's getting plenty of sleep, too.' Sophia smiled at the tiny, perfect face peeping from the folds of blanket in Judith's arms.

'I've been a bit worried about today's visit, though. I'm not sure I want her to have the test.' Judith's voice wobbled. 'It's going to hurt her, isn't it?'

'They usually cry,' Sophia said gently. 'But I think it's more about having their foot held still than any pain. It's a tiny prick. And the crying helps. It makes the blood come out faster so the test is over quickly.'

'It's important, Jude.' Their patient's mother was sitting nearby. She looked over at Sophia. 'There's all sorts of diseases it can test for, aren't there? Treatable things?'

'Absolutely. More than twenty different disorders, in fact.'

'Like what?'

'Maybe Flick can tell you about some of them.' Sophia smiled encouragingly at her student.

'There's hypothyroidism,' Flick said. 'And cystic fibrosis. And the enzyme disorders that prevent the normal use of milk.'

'And amino acid disorders,' Sophia added. 'Things

that can lead to something like brain damage if they're not picked up but which can be easily treated by following a special diet.'

'But she's not going to need a special diet for ages. I'm breastfeeding. Can't we put the test off until then?'

'It needs to be done as soon as possible after baby is forty-eight hours old.' Sophia checked her watch. 'And that's right about now.'

'I'll hold her, if you like,' Judith's mother offered. 'Why don't you go and have a quick shower or something?'

'No.' Judith closed her eyes. 'If it has to be done, I want to be the one holding her. Let's just get it over with.'

Flick stored the card with its four blood spots in Judith's file. 'I'd better remember to take that to the lab later,' she told Sophia as they drove to their next appointment. She shook her head. 'Poor Judith. I think she cried more than the baby did. Imagine how hard the six-week vaccinations are going to be for her.'

'Remind me to give her some pamphlets about that on our next visit. And we'll talk to her about how important it is.'

They had a hearing screening test to do on a final visit to a six-week-old baby later that morning and a lesson in hand-expressing breast milk for a young mother in the afternoon.

'I want my partner to share the night feeds,' she told them. 'And he really wants to, don't you, John?'

The young father nodded. The look and smile he gave his partner was exactly what Sophia would want for herself. Overflowing with love and a determination to provide support—even if it meant sacrificing sleep. Unaccountably, an image of Aiden filled her mind. How ridiculous was that? He was so against the idea of ever having a baby that he wouldn't trust anyone else to deal with contraception.

'But I really hate the thought of using one of those breast pumps,' the mother continued. 'It's so...mechanical.'

'Hand expression isn't hard. We'll show you how to do it.'

Flick took notes as Sophia provided the instruction. By the end of the day she'd also had plenty of practice taking blood pressures and temperatures on mothers, weighing babies and filling in report forms.

'You're getting very competent,' Sophia told her. 'You'll be doing all this on your own in no time.'

'Thanks. I'm loving it.' Flick opened her mouth as though about to say something else but then she merely smiled. 'See you tomorrow, Soph. Have a good night.'

Sophia smiled back. 'I intend to. You have one too.'

'Oh, man...that has to be the most amazing thing I've ever smelt.'

As an icebreaker, on opening the door to her dinner guest, this was enough to make Sophia smile and stop wondering about what was going to happen before or after they ate.

'Let's hope it tastes as good as it smells.' At least that was something she was pretty sure she didn't need to worry about. She'd been pretty impressed herself to come home to the aroma of those slow-cooked lamb shanks with red wine and mushrooms. The potatoes were cooking now and all she needed to do was mash them and dinner would be ready.

They had time to relax and, seeing as Aiden was holding out a bottle of very nice wine, it would have been rude not to taste it.

'Come in. I've got the fire going. It's pretty cold out there tonight, isn't it?'

'Sure is.' Aiden went straight to the flames of the small gas fire and stood with his back to it, his hand fanned out to catch the heat. He looked around. 'This is really nice.' His grin grew. 'Can't say I really noticed the other night.'

That grin—along with a ghost of a wink—chased away any lingering awkwardness over this date that wasn't a date. Suddenly, Sophia felt completely comfortable in his company. No, it was more than that. Being with him in this small, book-filled room with the smell of hot food and the sound of rain on the roof felt...well, it felt like *home*.

'It is nice, isn't it? Most of this stuff isn't mine, though. I'm house-sitting for a nurse at the Victoria who's gone overseas for a year. Sad to say, the year's half-over now. I'll have to start thinking about finding a place of my own before too long.'

'Where were you before this?' Aiden took the corkscrew Sophia handed him and dealt expertly with opening the wine while she took a couple of steps back into the kitchen to fetch glasses.

'Canberra. It's where I grew up.'

'You've got family there?' Aiden poured the wine.

'Just my parents. Dad's a pharmacist and Mum's a teacher.' Sophia sat down on the sofa and it felt good when Aiden came to sit beside her. 'How 'bout you?'

'No folks. There's just me and Nate. Mum died due to complications with his birth.'

'Oh…that's awful. Do you remember her?'

'Yeah…' For a second, Sophia could see the pain of that loss in his eyes but then his gaze slid sideways, as though he knew he might be revealing too much. 'Not as well as I'd like to, though. I was only six when she died.' He took a huge swallow of his wine.

Sophia's heart ached for the little boy who'd lost his mother. She'd never lost one of her maternity patients but she knew it still happened in rare cases and she could imagine how terrible it would be for the whole family.

'That smell is driving me mad.' Aiden's tone had a forced cheerfulness to it. An attempt to dispel any negative vibe? 'I didn't get time for lunch today.'

'Oh…' Maybe she couldn't do anything to comfort that little boy of years gone by but she could certainly fix this. 'Let's eat. Why don't you choose some music to put on while I mash the potatoes?'

His choice was surprising. 'You went for vinyl?'

'Retro, huh? The girl who owns this place is really into the old stuff.'

Sophia laughed. 'It's more like she's never thrown anything out. Dot's in her early sixties. At least you chose one of my favourites. I adore Cat Stevens.'

'Me, too.' Aiden took the plate from her hands but held her gaze. 'And how did you know that lamb shanks are my all-time favourite food?'

The warmth in that gaze made the pleasure of approval all the more intense and Sophia had to break the eye contact. 'Lucky guess. Or maybe we just have a lot in common.'

The food tasted just as good as it had smelled. The flames on the fake logs of the gas fire danced merrily and the music was the perfect background. All that was missing, Sophia decided, was candlelight.

Except wouldn't that make it too romantic to be a non-date? And what could she talk about that wouldn't take them into ground that might be deemed too personal and put it into the same category?

'You must have had a busy day, if you didn't get time for lunch.'

'Sure did. Two cardiac arrests, one straight after the other, would you believe?'

'Did you get them back?'

'Transported the first one with a viable rhythm but I think the downtime had been too long. The second guy woke up after the third shock and wanted to know what all the fuss was about.'

'No, really?'

'Yeah...' Aiden refilled their glasses and then raised his in a toast. 'Doesn't happen very often but when it does, it makes it all worthwhile. Even missing lunch.' He picked up his fork again. 'Did I tell you how amazing this is? I can't even mash potatoes without leaving lumps in.'

Sophia smiled. 'Tell me about the save. How old was he? Was there bystander CPR happening when you got there?'

Aiden told her about the successful case in so much detail she felt like she'd been standing there, watching the drama.

'You're really good at that.'

'What?'

'Telling a story. You could write a book about your job and people would want to read it.'

Aiden shook his head. 'I've just had practice, that's all. Nathan is a frustrated paramedic, I think. He always wants every gory detail about everything and doesn't let me get away with leaving stuff out. It's become a habit.'

Sophia forgot about any boundaries she might have been watching so that they could keep this time light. And fun. There was such a strong undercurrent to Aiden's words. It had the strength of showing the bond between the brothers in that Aiden was so used to sharing every detail of his life with Nathan, but it had rocks and rapids in it, too. Did Nathan resent that Aiden was out in the world, doing such an exciting and physical job, while he was trapped in a wheelchair? Did Aiden feel guilty about it?

'How did it happen?' she heard herself asking quietly. 'How did Nate become a quadriplegic?'

Aiden stopped chewing his mouthful of food and swallowed. Carefully. He reached for his glass of wine but didn't look at Sophia.

'He got pushed down a set of stairs.' His voice was flat.

'Oh, my God...' If she'd still had any appetite, it evaporated at that moment. 'How old was he?'

'Ten.'

A ten-year-old boy who'd probably loved to ride his bike and play soccer or rugby. A boy who'd already had it tough by having to grow up without his mother.

An echo of those sombre words Aiden had spoken the other night slipped into her head.

I had to be a father to Nate when he was growing up and that was enough. More than enough.

Had he been referring to the growing up before that dreadful accident or the trauma of readjustment that would have come afterwards?

She had so many questions she wanted to ask but didn't dare push further into such personal territory. The silence grew. Aiden was staring at his wineglass.

'Must have been drinking on such an empty stomach that did it,' he mused. 'I never talk about this.'

Then he looked up and caught Sophia's gaze. 'Or maybe it's because I'm with you.'

Something inside her melted into a liquid warmth. Some of it reached her eyes and she knew she'd have to blink a lot to make sure it didn't escape and roll down her cheeks. Her voice came out as a whisper.

'You can tell me anything. Or not. You're safe, either way.' She tried to smile but it didn't quite work.

Aiden wasn't smiling either. He felt like he was drowning in that moisture he could see collecting in Sophia's eyes. The *caring* behind them hit him like an emotional brick and tugged at something long forgotten. Poignant.

Did it remind him of the way his mother had looked at him, maybe?

'It was my father who pushed him down the stairs,' he found himself telling her. 'And it was my fault.'

The shock on her face was all too easy to read and Aiden cringed inwardly. He shouldn't have told her. She would think less of him. As little as he thought of himself?

But then her face changed. She looked like she was backing away even though she didn't move a single muscle.

'I don't believe that,' she said. 'Not one bit.'

How could she say that with such conviction? She barely knew him and she knew nothing of what had happened. A flash of anger made it easy to unchain words.

'My father was an alcoholic. He resented having to raise kids on his own and he blamed Nathan for causing Mum's death. He was a bully and he got really nasty when he was drinking, which was pretty much every day.'

The horror of that childhood was written all over Sophia's face. He could see it that way himself now, with the benefit of hindsight but, at the time, it had just been how things were.

'I knew how to handle him. I learned how to keep Nate safe. But that day? I was sixteen and I'd had enough. Instead of trying to defuse him, I flipped the coin. I started yelling at him and telling him just what a miserable bastard he was. I knew I had to get out of the house before I attacked him physically and I'd almost made it to the front door.' He had to stop for a second. To swallow past the constriction in his throat. 'He came after me but Nate was trying to follow me, too, and he was at the top of the stairs. Dad pushed him to get past and he fell.'

'You *saw* it happen?' Sophia's words were raw. Had she even thought before she reached out and covered his hand with her own? The warmth and pressure of that human contact almost undid Aiden but he couldn't pull his hand away. Instead, he turned it over and threaded his fingers through hers to lock them together.

'That wasn't the worst of it. I didn't know how badly hurt Nate was but I knew not to let him move before the ambulance could get there. So I held his head and kept him still and told him that everything would be okay. And then…and then…'

He could feel the tension in her hand. The terrible anticipation.

'And then we heard it. I didn't even know he had a gun in the house. Just as well, maybe, given how much I hated him that day. But I never had to think about killing him again. He did it himself.'

He choked on those last words. He'd never told anybody this story. Ever. Something was breaking inside his chest. Making him shake. Forcing a kind of horrible, dry sobbing sound to come out of his throat. He had his eyes screwed tightly shut so he didn't see Sophia standing up but he felt the tug on his hand and it was easy to comply with the silent instruction because he had no idea of what to do. How to deal with this awful emotional tidal wave.

How did Sophia know what to do?

She was tiny but he could feel an enormous strength

in the way she wrapped her arms around him and held him so tightly. He had no idea how long they stood there like that but it was long enough for the wave to recede. And now it felt like a huge expanse of sand that had been washed clean.

Deserted. And amazingly peaceful.

He loosened the grip of his arms around Sophia. How had she managed to keep breathing for so long?

'Sorry. I shouldn't have dumped all that on you.'

'I'm glad you did.' She moved a little in his arms so that she could look up at him. 'And, Aiden?'

'Yeah?'

'I was right.'

'What about?'

'It wasn't your fault. Not one bit of it.'

The anger was gone but he could still feel disappointed. Sophia was taking Nathan's side. Was there nobody out there who could understand? See the truth the way he saw it? He stepped back. Could he make some excuse and simply leave?

No. One look at Sophia and he was caught.

'I know why you think that,' she said. 'And when you love someone, it's easy to find a way to take the blame when something bad happens to them, but this wasn't your fault. It was your father's fault.'

'I *provoked* him.'

'And how many times did you *not* provoke him? You'd been living with that for ten years. You'd found every way under the sun to keep your little brother safe. Confronting your father and escaping would have been the only way to make sure of that in the long run and I think you'd finally got old enough to know that, even if it was subconscious. Okay, it went horribly wrong but it was a brave thing to do. How old were you?'

'Sixteen.' Aiden could barely get the word out. He was trying to process what she was saying. Was there any truth in it?

He'd been *brave*?

No way...

'There you go.' Sophia's smile was heartbreakingly tender. 'Just a kid yourself.' She raised her eyebrows. 'Was that when you decided you wanted to be a para-medic?'

'Yeah... They were amazing. I think they looked after me just as much as they looked after Nate. It's some-thing I have in the back of my mind with every job I go to. It's not just the person who's sick or hurt that's your patient. The people who love them are too.'

'And that's part of what makes you so good at your job. No wonder Nate wants to hear your stories.'

That was how this had all started, wasn't it. Aiden jerked his gaze to the table. To the half-eaten meals of that delicious food Sophia had prepared.

'I'm sorry,' he said again. 'I kind of ruined dinner, didn't I?'

'It was my fault,' Sophia said. 'I asked the questions that got you started.'

'I didn't have to tell you. I chose to. Because I wanted to.'

The look he was receiving could only have come from a woman.

'Mmm...okay. I accept that it wasn't my fault.'

In the heartbeat of silence that followed, Aiden made the connection. And found himself smiling, albeit reluctantly.

'How 'bout I zap those plates in the microwave? You still hungry?'

He couldn't look away from her eyes. He was drowning again but this time it came with a lick of fire that would evaporate any moisture.

'Oh, yeah…I'm hungry.'

He caught her hand as she turned towards the table.

'But not for food.'

She gave a tiny gasp as he pulled her into his arms and bent his head to taste her lips. And then she melted against him and he knew, with absolute certainty, that things were going to be all right. He didn't have to leave. Didn't want to.

Things were going to be better than all right, in fact.

Life itself seemed to have just become that much better.

CHAPTER EIGHT

This was nothing like last time.

Oh, the desire was the same. That being carried away on a wave of physical sensation that led to ultimate satisfaction, but there was something very different about the way Sophia could feel herself responding.

This physical nakedness had come in the wake of emotional nakedness on Aiden's part. He'd opened his heart to her and made himself vulnerable and it made her want to protect him, even as her own heart broke to think of what his childhood had been like. Weird how it could break but swell at the same time as she saw the depth of the love he had for his brother.

No wonder he shied away from any other responsibilities in his life—like a relationship that lasted more than three dates. Or having a child of his own.

And the guilt he'd carried with him ever since that accident. Was it more than not wanting extra responsibilities? Was he preventing anyone else getting too close as a kind of penance?

She'd told him he was safe to tell her anything and he had. Way more than she'd expected.

He deserved the same kind of honesty from her. To know that he was safe from more than any emotional repercussions of being close, but something stopped her saying anything when he tore open the foil packet of the condom.

It would spoil the moment, she told herself. Bring the rush of escalating desire to a grinding halt and maybe it was more than simply desire for Aiden at the moment. Maybe he needed the intimacy as a kind of reassurance. A reminder that he deserved the good things in life because of who he was.

The good things in life.

Like being loved...

No. Sophia had to shut down the realisation because it was blinding. And terrifying. Far easier to stop thinking and simply feel. To give herself up to the touch of Aiden's hands and mouth. To give in to her own need to feel the closest physical touch possible from another being.

It came back, though, in those quiet minutes of lying there entangled in each other's arms, as heart and breathing rates gradually settled back to normal.

No. This was nothing like last time. Because this had been more than sex. More than having fun. On her part, it had been making love.

Aiden had opened his heart to her and she had fallen into it. Fallen in love with him.

This wasn't supposed to have happened. How could it, when you knew right from the start that it was only going to last for three dates?

* * *

He'd fallen asleep.

He hadn't meant to. He never stayed a whole night because it was one of the rules. He'd learned long ago that it added a depth that made things more difficult when it was time to move on because it gave the impression that he might be happy to stay longer. That it was about more than a bit of fun.

He'd taken the fun element out of the evening himself, though, hadn't he? Spilling his guts like that about Nate. About his father.

Good grief...he'd never told a woman any of that stuff.

But she'd told him it was safe and nobody had ever said that to him before.

And he'd *felt* safe.

He'd even felt...absolved from the guilt for just a heartbeat. The way she'd twisted the idea of being at fault and tipped it towards being someone else's choice.

There was a truth in that. Maybe he'd be able to catch that feeling of absolution again one day. It had been too huge not to push away at the time, though. To shut off everything except the need to take Sophia to bed. To try and thank her for what she'd given him? It wasn't surprising he'd fallen asleep after the roller-coaster of emotions that had been stirred up and then released. Physical release had been the last push into a totally new feeling of being at peace.

Safe.

Such a roller-coaster. Like that extraordinary sensation he'd had when she'd told him he'd been brave.

Brave?

She admired him? Remembering it now gave him that same weird feeling of being...what...special? But she didn't know the truth of it, did she? How scared he'd been so often. The way he'd taken Nathan under his bed sometimes and held the toddler close until he'd known that his father had been drunk enough to be no threat for the rest of the night. How he'd stolen money from their dad's wallet so he could buy a toy for Nate's birthday. How often he'd wagged school or lied about being sick so that he could make sure the housekeeper was taking proper care of his brother.

She wouldn't think he was brave if she'd known the awful relief he'd felt when it had become clear after the accident that Nathan would have to be cared for by people far more qualified than he was. That all he needed to do was visit him every day. That he was free to follow the dream that had been born on that dreadful night and become a paramedic so he could help others.

He'd created exactly the life he'd dreamed of but he had hurt other people along the way, he knew that. Some women in the past had been angry. Had accused him of using them. Others had been upset and the tears had been harder to handle than angry words.

How would Sophia react when they'd had their third—and last—date?

The last thing he wanted was to make her cry.

Even thinking about it made him hold her a little tighter as she lay in his arms, with her head tucked against his chest. The movement made her stir and make a tiny sound, almost like a cat purring.

He loved that sound.

'Mmm.' This was more like a word and it was followed by a slow, deep indrawn breath that was painted into sensation by the small hand that moved across his chest.

'You're still here,' Sophia whispered. 'That's nice.'

'Mmm.' He had to agree. It *was* nice.

'What time is it?'

'I don't know. Close to dawn, I think. The birds are getting noisy.'

'We don't have to get up yet, though.' Her hand was moving again. The soft touch reached his abdomen and Aiden could feel his body coming a lot more awake.

'We don't.' Okay, maybe this wasn't the best idea but how could he resist? 'Just as well I came prepared this time.' His jeans weren't far away. There was another foil packet in the back pocket.

He couldn't miss the way Sophia stilled in his arms, though. The way the fuzzy sense of sleepy peacefulness took on a spiky edge.

'What?' The word was no more than a puzzled murmur. Had he done the wrong thing in being prepared for more than once?

'I...' The hesitation lasted long enough for Sophia to take another deep breath. He could feel the press of her breast against his hand swell and then recede. 'I meant what I said the other night. You don't need it.'

Whoa... This was a step into totally forbidden territory. He didn't care what precautions any woman took. He had to know he was taking responsibility for contraception himself.

The desire for sex was ebbing fast. He needed to escape. Carefully, he started pulling his arm away from
where it encircled Sophia but he had no idea what he
could say. How he could stop this becoming an unpleasant conversation for both of them.

But he didn't have to find anything to say because
Sophia spoke first.

'I can't get pregnant, Aiden. I had a hysterectomy
nearly ten years ago.'

'What? *Why?*' Oh, God...had she had cancer? The
idea that she'd had to face something so terrible at such
a young age was unbearable. Instead of taking his arm
away, Aiden found himself pushing it further around
her. Pulling her closer, as if he could protect her from
something.

'It was an accidental pregnancy.' Her voice was quiet.
Matter-of-fact. 'It was ectopic but I ignored the early
warning signs. It went on too long and then ruptured
really badly. They had to perform a hysterectomy to
control the bleeding.'

Aiden swore softly, his eyes tightly shut. He could
imagine all too easily the emergency that rupture would
have caused. The urgent, major surgery that would have
been necessary to save her life. But...

'But why did you ignore the signs?'

It seemed a long time before she spoke again and
when she did, her voice was so quiet he barely heard it.

'I wanted the baby,' she said.

That took a few moments to process. 'How old were
you?'

'Twenty-one. I was a student midwife. I'd always

loved babies. Maybe because I was an only child and I was so envious when my best friend got a baby sister. My parents both worked full time and it felt like we were...I don't know...less of a family, I guess.'

'But you said the pregnancy was accidental.'

'Of course it was. I wasn't stupid. I was only twenty-one and it wasn't as if the relationship was going anywhere. We were both young. Just out to have a bit of fun.'

Like he was with the women in his life? Aiden had to swallow a nasty pang of guilt. Those women had had every right to be angry or upset, hadn't they? He *had* been using them.

'So he wasn't keen on the idea of being a father?'

'He did his best to be supportive but we both knew it couldn't have worked. I actually went down the track of having a termination but when I went to ring up to make an appointment, I couldn't do it. I realised then that I wanted that baby. I...I already loved it.' There was a wobble in her voice. 'So I ignored the abdominal pain that came and went. I told myself that a bit of bleeding could be perfectly normal in the early stages of some pregnancies. That things would settle down once I got to the end of the first trimester and I'd go and get checked out and have a scan after that. When it was less likely that anyone would try and talk me into getting rid of it.'

'And then it ruptured.'

'I was about fourteen weeks by then. I guess it was lucky it happened while I was at work. I might have bled out pretty fast if I'd been anywhere else.'

'I'm glad you were at work, then. Lucky for me, too.'

A tiny sound that could have been an embryonic sob

came from Sophia but then they were both silent for a long time.

'I'm sorry,' Aiden said, finally, into the light of a new day that was filtering through the gap in the curtains. 'You lost something huge and it must have been devastating.' Not only had she lost the baby she'd already loved but she'd lost the chance of ever having another one.

'Yeah…it was tough but that's just the way it is. I'm not going to let it define me. I'm going to make the best of my life. This isn't a practice run, you know? It's the only life we get.'

She reminded him of Nathan. Totally different things to deal with, of course. Or were they so different? Nathan lived with the loss of mobility. He'd had to come to terms with a different perception of his body and where he was going in life.

Sophia lived with the loss of a dream. Wouldn't being unable to ever be a mother involve the same sort of process in coming to terms with that different perception and direction?

The similarity was there. Perhaps the greatest similarity was in the positive attitude to making the best of his life.

He was so proud of his brother's attitude. He loved him to the point where it made his chest ache.

And right now he was feeling a very similar pride in Sophia.

A similar kind of love?

Oh, man…that was a scary thought. He'd never actually fallen in love with a woman. He'd known to get out as soon as there were any warning signs. Had he ignored them for some reason this time?

He tried to search his memory.

Had it been the first time he'd seen her smile? Or when he'd heard her laugh—way back, when they'd first met and she'd introduced herself as being a midwife and he'd joked that he hoped *she* was, given the emergency cord prolapse she'd just dealt with.

No. That had simply been attraction. No danger signs that could have been spotted there.

What about that first date, though? When he'd seen her at the door of that crowded bar? The way the noise of the people and music had just faded away until it had felt like he and Sophia were the only people on the planet?

Yeah...maybe that should have rung an alarm bell, given that it had never happened before.

And she'd loved his three-dates rule. Maybe that was the problem. She'd made him feel safe.

Or maybe it was the way she'd made him feel safe last night. Safe enough to tell her anything.

He couldn't tell her what he was feeling right now. No way.

She'd said that a three-dates rule was exactly what was missing from *her* life. She didn't want the complications of a long-term relationship. She couldn't have a family so maybe it simply wasn't a part of her life plan now.

She wouldn't want to know how he was feeling. It might make her feel bad when she walked away from him to get on with the life that wasn't a practice run.

He didn't want her to feel bad.

He'd make her feel good instead.

Her lips were easy to find. Soft and deliciously responsive. They still had time, didn't they?

This would be a first for him. Sex without protection, but Sophia had shown him something that made her vulnerable and she deserved at least the reassurance of trust.

And...man, it made things feel different.

Nothing like the last time.

Nothing like any time. Ever.

The text message on Aiden's phone came when he was on the point of leaving her house to go to work.

The atmosphere was a little odd. Sophia thought it was because they'd come out to find the remnants of last night's dinner still on the table and it had been a shock. So much had happened since they'd been sitting there.

So much had changed between them?

Yes. The atmosphere was strange. As if they both realised how huge that change had been and it was making them both nervous.

So much for having fun. A limited amount of time to enjoy each other's company. Some 'no-strings' sex.

'I could help clean up,' Aiden offered.

'No. I've got more time than you. I don't start till eight. You've only got ten minutes if you want to get to the station in time to start at seven.'

'Okay. But next time I'm doing the dishes.'

Next time?

Was that going to be date number three or would it still be a non-date if they didn't go out anywhere? Sophia found herself smiling. On the point of clarifying the 'rules' again when the text message bleeped.

That was even more of a shock than the messy table had been. Not that there was someone else who wanted to make contact so early in the day but the way it made Sophia feel.

Jealous?

'It's only Nate,' Aiden said after a glance at his phone. 'I'll call him when I get to work.'

He kissed her goodbye and once again Sophia found herself listening to the sound of his bike roaring away.

No. That feeling hadn't been jealousy. It was deeper than that. She'd known it was probably his brother rather than another woman who was texting him and that made her remember that he had another part of his life that was more important than any woman could ever be to him.

Another part of his life that would swallow him without a ripple when she was no longer a consideration.

Oh, help... If she could feel this bleak before it had even ended, how bad was it going to be when they said goodbye at the end of date number three?

But did it have to end?

Aiden didn't want to have kids.

She *couldn't* have any.

She'd avoided serious relationships because she had less to offer than most women but Aiden didn't want what she didn't have to offer anyway.

Didn't that make them perfect for each other?

The thought came with a leap of something that felt like hope and Sophia found herself holding it as she took plates to the kitchen sink, scraped off the abandoned food and rinsed them clean.

Who would have thought that she might find a man who could not only accept that she couldn't have a baby but would welcome it?

Except that something didn't feel right about this picture. The pieces didn't quite fit. Or maybe there were some missing that were leaving a hole she couldn't identify.

A wipe down of the table obliterated any reminder of last night's meal and Sophia collected her bag and coat to set off on her walk to the Victoria.

She couldn't shake the feeling that something was wrong, however.

That she was too far along a track for turning around to be possible. That she might be heading for some kind of crash and there was nothing at all she could do to prevent it.

CHAPTER NINE

WHAT WAS A girl to do when she couldn't figure out what it was that was bothering her?

Talk about it, of course. To someone she knew she could trust. Someone who knew more about her than anyone and loved her enough to want to help her figure it out.

Her mum?

Sadly, for Sophia, that couldn't be her first port of call. The love was there but the depth of understanding wasn't. Even after all these years, the relief her mother hadn't been able to hide when she'd lost her baby was hurtful.

'It would have ruined your life, being a single mother,' she'd said. 'Your career would have gone out the window and there aren't many men who really want to take on raising someone else's child.'

But she'd loved that baby. That potential little person to love and be loved by. Her career had seemed far less important in comparison.

'There are worse things than not having children.' Had her mother really thought she was offering comfort? 'You're about to be qualified to do the job you've always wanted to do. Focus on that. It'll make you happy.'

Had it been her mother's job that had made *her* happy? Had it been a mistake to have a child at all? One that would have ruined her life if she'd become pregnant accidentally before she had established her career or found a husband?

If it had been a mistake, her parents hid it well and had done the best job they could in raising their child, but that childhood had been a lonely one. There had clearly never been the possibility of siblings and with both her parents working full time, even a family dog had been ruled out as company.

Which was why it had been such a joy to spend time at home with her best friend, Emily, ever since she'd first arrived in Melbourne. To soak in the chaos of an extended family that included an adorably woolly, brown dog by the name of Fuzzy.

With her next day off coinciding with one of Em's, it was a no-brainer to invite herself for a visit and a chance to talk to the person most likely to be able to identify what it was that was bothering her so much.

They were in the garden of Emily and Oliver's house. Well, the house actually belonged to Em's mother, Adrianna, but it was the family home for them all now. And the family was growing, despite the sadness of losing Emily's foster-daughter, Gretta, a few weeks ago.

'How's it working out, having Ruby here with you?'

'Couldn't be better.' Emily lifted two-year-old Toby from his tricycle and took him to sit under the tree. 'I wish she'd rest a bit more, though. Look—she's over there, pruning roses. It's not that long since the in utero surgery on her baby.'

As if sensing she was being discussed, the waif-like teenager looked across the garden and waved at the two women.

'Am I doing it right?' she called. 'I've never tried this before.'

'You're doing a great job,' Emily called back. 'But you don't have to.'

The shy grin in response came with a shrug that was pure teenager.

'She feels like she has to help out,' Emily told Sophia, 'because we're not charging her any rent for the bungalow. And Mum wouldn't let her help with any housework this afternoon. Said it could wait till tomorrow because she felt like putting her feet up and reading her book. I'd rather Ruby was reading a book, too. She could be doing a bit of study or something so that she feels ready to go back to school after the baby comes.'

'I'm sure she will, when she gets used to being here. It must be a big thing, feeling like she's part of a family.'

Emily's smile was that of a contented woman as she nodded, watching Toby doing his stiff-legged crawl towards Sophia.

'Huge,' she agreed quietly.

Toby stopped and held up his arms. Sophia gladly gathered him onto her lap and let the toddler bury his head against her shoulder as he settled in for a cuddle. The faded blue kangaroo toy in his other hand felt a bit damp against the back of her neck.

'That's Kanga, isn't it? Gretta's toy?'

'Mmm.' Emily's smile grew misty. 'He's barely let it go since we lost her. I don't think he understands that she died but he's missing her.'

Toby's curls were springy and too irresistible not to stroke. An African child, Toby had been brought to Australia so that he could receive treatment for his spinal deformity and the scarring on his face from infection.

'How's it going with the adoption process?'

Emily groaned. 'The paperwork is endless. Ollie's confident that we'll get there, though. He says not getting there simply isn't an option.'

Her smile was proud now. Full of love for the man she 'remarried' so recently.

For a long moment, Sophia focused on the gorgeous cuddle she was receiving. Then her gaze drifted over Toby's head to where Ruby was eyeing up another rose bush, rubbing her back as she straightened.

'Do you remember when Ruby was waking up after the operation on the baby?'

'Of course.'

'What we were talking about?'

'Josh?'

'Mmm.' Josh. The baby Emily had lost at twenty-eight weeks—about the stage that Ruby was in her pregnancy now. The one successful round of all the IVF Emily and Oliver had gone through. 'After that. About why you and Oliver had split up.'

'Because he couldn't face adopting a baby?'

'He'd been adopted himself, hadn't he? And it hadn't been happy?'

'Mmm.'

'But he really wants to adopt Toby now, doesn't he?'

'Even more than I do, I think. Although that's not really possible. Hey, Toby…it's about my turn for a cuddle, isn't it?'

Obligingly, Toby crawled off Sophia's lap and threw himself at Emily with a joyful crow.

'Mumma!'

Even more obligingly, Fuzzy slithered closer and put his head on Sophia's lap so that she still had a head to stroke.

'You wanted kids so much,' she said quietly. 'You weren't going to let infertility stop you. And look what you've got now. A whole family, including a husband who adores you.'

'I'm the luckiest woman in the world,' Emily agreed.

'But you did it anyway, even without Oliver, and you were still happy, weren't you?'

'Ye-es…' Emily peered around Toby's head to give her friend a searching look. 'Where's this coming from, Soph? Is something bothering you?'

Sophia nodded. 'I'm not sure what it is. But I remember being at your vow renewal ceremony and thinking how brave you were. And that I needed to get braver too. Make changes in my life so that I could find something as good as what you've found. I even thought I could maybe try fostering or adopting kids one day, too.'

'You have made changes.' Emily's smile was encouraging. 'It's going well with that gorgeous boyfriend of yours, isn't it?'

'It's almost over,' Sophia told her. 'He has a three-dates rule.'

'A *what*?'

'He only ever goes out on three dates with a woman. That way you can have fun but it doesn't get heavy, you know?'

'No.' Emily shook her head. 'You've been out on more than three dates, haven't you?'

'Hmm. The rules got bent a bit. One of them was finishing off a date that got interrupted. And one wasn't really a date because he came to my place and we didn't go out anywhere.'

Emily laughed. 'Sounds like the rule isn't a real rule at all. I wouldn't worry about it.' She frowned. 'In fact, I don't like it. Sounds like an easy escape route for a commitment-phobe to me.'

'Yeah…well, I told him I liked the rule a lot, the first time we went out. That I was only after a bit of fun, too. Nothing serious.'

'Ohh…' Emily gave her another searching look. 'You've fallen for him, haven't you?'

'Yeah…' The word was a sigh. 'The weird thing is that, on paper, we're perfect for each other. I can't have kids and he doesn't want any.'

'Really? Why not?'

Sophia closed her eyes for a long moment, drawn back instantly to that night when Aiden had bared his soul to her and told her things he'd never told anyone. He'd trusted her.

And, yes, Emily knew all about her own story but that was hers to tell. She couldn't share Aiden's. Couldn't break that trust. But there were parts that weren't as private as an abusive childhood with an alcoholic father. Or the guilt of feeling responsible for a dreadful accident.

'He's got a brother. Nathan. He's a quadriplegic. Aiden's more than a big brother to him. He's like a parent, too, I guess. A whole family. I think he's got an unwritten rule about not letting anything interfere with that responsibility.'

'Wow...' Emily was silent for a minute. 'Does he feel the same way about you?'

'I don't know. I think he's let me into his life more than he ever has with any other woman. I've met Nathan. We went to a Murderball game.'

'Is that the wheelchair rugby?'

'Yes. It's really exciting to watch. And Nathan's cool. I really like him. He lives in sheltered accommodation but he seems to have his life pretty well sorted. He's got a girlfriend who has more facial piercings than I've ever seen and they clearly adore each other.'

Sophia was rubbing Fuzzy's head and pulling gently on his ears. She bent her own head, horrified that she could feel tears gathering. It was great to be talking to Emily but she didn't want to spoil a lovely afternoon by falling to pieces. What was wrong with her?

'Oh, hon...' Emily's voice was full of sympathy. 'You've got it bad, haven't you?'

The nod dislodged a tear. She swiped it away.

'I don't know what I'm so upset about. I knew it was never supposed to last more than three dates and the next one has got to count for number three. We can't keep bending his silly rule for ever.'

'That's not the real problem, though, is it?'

Sophia swallowed. 'Isn't it?'

Emily shook her head. She tickled Toby, making him chortle, and then pulled him closer for another hug. 'I think it goes deeper than that.'

'In what way?'

'You're not really perfect for each other. Paper doesn't count.' Emily's gaze was serious now. 'Aiden doesn't want kids. And maybe he has good reason for that. But you do want them, even if you've tried to convince yourself you didn't for all these years. You probably want that as much as I did. You want a real family and you know it's quite possible to have that, even if you can't give birth to your own babies. Look at me.'

'I know.' Sophia drew in a long, slow breath as she found herself nodding slowly.

Yes. That was it, in a nutshell. What had been niggling away in the back of her mind. Aiden didn't want children. And she did. It could never work.

End of story?

Maybe not.

'But Oliver didn't want to adopt children either and look at him, now—leading the crusade to let you keep Toby in the country.'

'He didn't want to adopt,' Emily agreed, 'but he always wanted to be a father. It's a bit different.' It was her turn to sigh. 'Life's an unfair business sometimes, isn't it?'

Toby had crawled off Emily's lap now and was heading towards Ruby. Fuzzy abandoned Sophia and went after Toby like a sheepdog looking after his charge. Ruby grinned as she saw them coming. She bent to pick Toby up but then froze. Something about her posture made both Emily and Sophia share an alarmed glance.

'Ruby?' Emily was on her feet in a flash. 'What's wrong?'

It was too quiet today.

So much easier to silence an annoyingly persistent voice in the back of your head if you could keep busy. Even better if you had a real challenge to rise to.

What Aiden needed was something dramatic. A cardiac arrest, maybe—one that led to a successful outcome, of course. Or some trauma. A crush injury perhaps, that would need careful management, especially if whatever was doing the crushing was still in place. A prang would do. A mess of two or three vehicles with an unknown number of potential injuries and the chaos of disrupted traffic and impatient onlookers creating difficulty for any emergency personnel to get to the scene. He'd get there first and get to do the scene management and triage, which was always a challenge of unknown quantity.

But no. What he had was an elderly homeless guy in central Melbourne suffering from double pneumonia. He was sitting just under a bridge beside the popular walking track that led to Southbank. Apparently, he'd been sitting there for the last three days so people had eventually noticed that he had barely moved. Finally, a concerned pedestrian had called the police. The police had called the ambulance service for a medical assessment. They knew this man and knew he didn't talk much. Asking questions wasn't going to solve anything.

'His name's Bruce,' they told Aiden. 'But that's all we know about him, other than that he's been living on the streets for years. Him and his dog.'

The dog looked as old and thin and unkempt as his owner and seemed happy to sit just as immobile, with his head on Bruce's lap. It seemed to know that Aiden was trying to help but growled ominously if any of the police came too close.

After an initial assessment, Aiden had called for transport so now he was just keeping Bruce company. He had his patient on oxygen and a foil survival blanket was wrapped around his shoulders. He'd taken a baseline set of vital signs. Blood pressure was too low, temperature too high. The respiration rate was way too high and blood-oxygen level way too low. Even with the mask on and oxygen coming from the small cylinder he carried on the bike, there had been little improvement over the last ten minutes. Bruce's lips were still blue and he could almost hear the crackle in his lungs without using a stethoscope.

Where on earth was the back-up for transport? Had they been diverted to exactly the kind of drama he was desperate for himself? Something that would stop the argument in his head that was gaining momentum—on both sides.

He couldn't even talk to the two police officers who had moved a safe distance away from the dog and seemed to see something on the river that was interesting enough to keep them chatting.

He only had Bruce, who didn't talk. And a sad-looking dog who was going to look even sadder when they had to take his master away in the ambulance. The police had called a pet shelter that was sending a rescue crew to help. Aiden doubted that these two would ever be reunited and that sucked.

'I'm sorry about this,' he told Bruce quietly, crouching beside him and checking that the oxygen saturation probe was still covering a finger. 'But we have to take you somewhere you can be warm and comfortable so the antibiotics have a chance to work.'

He took Bruce's heart and respiration rate again, just for something to do, but it felt wrong to be so silent. The noise of the city was a distant hum. The sound of voices and laughter came occasionally as a pair of joggers or cyclists went past on the track but the snippets of normality vanished as quickly as they came. He had to talk to Bruce even if the old man couldn't respond or possibly didn't even understand. But what could he talk about? He'd only had one thing on his mind for the last couple of days.

'I'd like to go out tonight,' he found himself telling Bruce. Still quietly enough for nobody but the dog to overhear. 'But, at the same time, I don't want to because if I do, it's going to be the last date I have with this girl and that would be a real shame because she's…well… she's perfect, that's what she is.'

The perfect woman for him, at any rate.

He never wanted to have children.

Sophia couldn't ever have children.

And hadn't that vow to never take on the responsibility of a family of his own been the whole basis of the three-dates rule? To get out before he fell in love? Before she fell in love with him and wanted more—like living together or getting married? Before her biological clock started ticking more and more loudly and the desire to have a baby became the priority?

But he'd never been on this side of the equation. Never been the one who didn't want things to end.

Sophia had welcomed the rule. She didn't want anything long term either. And why would she? She wasn't planning on having a family any more than he was so she wouldn't see herself in the role of a mother. Or a wife.

Someone was going to get hurt and Aiden had the horrible feeling it was going to be him.

Could they stay friends, perhaps, after their official dating period was over?

Friends with benefits even?

No. As if that could work.

As if it could ever be enough.

'I didn't get out in time.' The words came out like a sigh of defeat and triggered a move to check his watch. Where on earth was that back-up? He could hear a siren in the distance but that wouldn't be the crew coming to transport his patient because the job wouldn't have been assigned the urgency of needing lights and sirens. It would be well down the list and probably getting bumped repeatedly as calls came in for more serious incidents.

A glance towards the police officers showed them to be in deep conversation now. Maybe they were enjoying the enforced break from their duties. Life still flowed along the track beside them. A young mother was jogging as she pushed a twin stroller that had a toddler on one side and a baby cocoon strapped on the other. Behind her, an older couple walked hand in hand, and as Aiden watched they turned to each other and shared a smile. In his peripheral vision he saw Bruce move, too. A tiny movement of just his hand as it rested on the dog's head. One finger moving to gently rub a floppy ear.

Something inside Aiden twisted painfully. That dog was probably the only living thing that Bruce had a relationship with. Responsibility for. And, any moment now, someone was going to turn up with a van to take the dog away.

'They'll take good care of him,' Aiden said. 'There are families out there who love to foster dogs.'

Was it his imagination or was Bruce's level of consciousness slipping further? He put his hand on the old man's wrist to feel for a pulse. The dog nudged his hand with a cold nose and that twisting sensation in his gut intensified.

It wasn't just about whether or not you could have kids, was it? Responsibility came with any relationship if you wanted to do the best you could and Aiden had never taken anything on without making sure he did his absolute best.

He was the best paramedic he could be.

The best brother.

When you loved somebody enough, their happiness became as important as your own. More important, maybe. Nathan's happiness had always been more important than his own. Right now, it felt like Sophia's happiness was important, too.

He wanted her to be happy.

He wanted to be the one to *make* her happy.

But if he was really honest, he wanted to be happy himself and that was why this was so damned hard.

Sophia didn't want more than three dates so he couldn't throw the rule book away. And that meant that if he wanted to see her again, it would be for the last time.

And *that* meant he would never see her again.

Did that mean he *didn't* want the date even more than he did want it?

Two men were coming along the track now, carrying a wire crate between them. They wore overalls with the logo of the animal rescue service. Not far behind them, an ambulance crew was wheeling a stretcher. The police officers noted the arrival of assistance and started to move closer in case they were needed.

The wait was over.

The speed with which things were sorted seemed almost indecent after the long wait. Surprisingly, the dog didn't protest at being bundled into the crate and Bruce seemed equally defeated—barely conscious as he was lifted to the stretcher and covered with warm blankets. After handing over his paperwork to the ambulance crew, the last thing Aiden needed to do was change the oxygen supply and take his own small cylinder back to the bike.

'All the best, Bruce,' he said. 'I'll keep an eye out for you next time I'm down this way.'

The old man's eyes opened slowly. His lips moved. Aiden lifted the mask.

'Ask her,' Bruce mumbled. 'Tell her...'

Oh, man... It was a cringe-worthy moment to realise

that he'd been heard and understood when he'd been sharing something so decidedly unprofessional. Aiden didn't want to have to think about it and, lucky for him, he didn't have to. He'd barely got his helmet back on his head when a priority call came through to an address in Brunswick.

'Premature labour,' he was told. 'Approximately twenty-eight weeks gestation. Mother seventeen years old. Nearest ambulance is at least ten minutes away.'

Aiden kicked his bike into life and flicked on the beacons. Anticipation was tinged with relief. This was exactly what he needed.

Drama. A life—other than his own—that was hanging in the balance.

'The ambulance is on its way.'

'How long?' Sophia was kneeling behind Ruby, holding the girl in her arms to support her.

'I don't *want* an ambulance,' Ruby sobbed. 'I just want this to *stop*. It *hurts*…'

'I know, sweetheart.' Sophia tightened her hug. 'But sometimes it's baby who decides when things are going to happen.' She turned to catch Emily's gaze and mouthed her question again silently.

Emily held up the fingers of both hands and her look said it all. Ten minutes could well be too long. She tilted her head towards the house with her eyebrows raised but Sophia had to shake her head. They'd already tried to get Ruby inside but she'd been almost hysterical as the first pain had hit and her waters had broken. She'd frozen and then collapsed onto the ground when Emily and Sophia had taken her arms to help her walk.

Emily's mother, Adrianna, came rushing out of the house with an armload of blankets. 'I'll keep Toby in with me,' she said. 'Where on earth is that ambulance? We called them ages ago.'

'It was only a few minutes, Mum,' Emily said. 'And I can hear a siren.'

'Oh...thank goodness.' Adrianna tucked a blanket around Ruby's shoulders. 'You'll be okay now, love. You'll be safely in hospital in no time.'

'I won't,' Ruby sobbed. 'It's too early. I didn't think I wanted this baby but I do...I want it *so* much...'

'I know.' Sophia kept hugging her. She knew how it felt to be faced with the fear of losing an unborn baby you'd already fallen in love with. She also knew that Ruby's fears were justified. This was far too early—especially if this baby was going to arrive before they had the benefit of all the resuscitation gear that the MMU would have on hand. Emily was looking desperately worried and that was enough to pull Sophia even further from the calm, professional space she was trying to hang onto.

And that siren sounded...different?

It wasn't really a surprise to see the big bike pulling in to the side of the road and a helmeted figure opening panniers to grab equipment.

What was surprising was the way her fear seemed to evaporate the moment she saw that it was Aiden who had responded to the call.

'The ambulance isn't far away,' he told Ruby, as he crouched beside her. 'I'm just the advance party.' He looked up to include all of them. 'Tell me what's happening. How far apart are the contractions?'

Emily filled him in on the sudden start of Ruby's labour. She also told him that the baby had had in utero surgery a few weeks ago to correct spina bifida and that Ruby had been kept on complete bed rest until they had been confident she wouldn't go into labour. By the time she finished speaking, the ambulance had arrived.

'We'll get you into the ambulance,' Aiden said. 'But we'll need to check where we're at before we roll.'

'I'm coming too,' Emily said.

There would be no room in the ambulance for Sophia to go as well but she went as far as the ambulance and waited while Aiden and Emily examined Ruby. Everything seemed under control but suddenly Ruby cried out as another contraction hit and then nothing was under control. Within seconds Aiden was holding a tiny scrap of a baby in his hands.

'Soph? Open that kit for me and get the ziplock bag.'

Her hands were shaking as she complied. She knew to wrap preterm infants in bubble wrap but a plastic bag? The baby wasn't making any sound and this was not looking good.

But Aiden seemed to know exactly what he was doing. He cut and clamped the cord and then put the baby into the bag leaving the head outside.

'Dry the head for me,' he told Emily. 'And cover it with a corner of the blanket. Soph—can you bring that airway kit a bit closer, please?'

One of the ambulance crew got there first and Sophia edged further away. The back of the ambulance was crowded now and all Emily could do was hold Ruby's hand and try to reassure her as she watched what was happening with the baby.

Sophia stood pressed against the open back door of the ambulance. She couldn't look away from that fierce concentration on Aiden's face. He was invested in this job a thousand per cent, determined to succeed, and she loved him for that.

And she felt so proud of him. That he knew exactly what to do and that he was doing it with such confidence and skill.

His hands moved so fast. They looked huge against the tiny pieces of equipment, like the smallest ever size of a laryngoscope blade and breathing tube. The ventilation bag was also tiny and he was squeezing it so gently to deliver such small puffs of oxygen.

'Hook up the monitor,' he told one of the crew. 'I need continuous monitoring of end tidal CO_2.'

The baby still wasn't moving but Aiden wasn't starting any chest compressions. His gaze was flicking between the baby and the monitor.

'Heart rate's over sixty,' he said. 'Let's roll. I want to get this little girl into NICU asap.'

Sophia had to step back so that the doors could be slammed shut. Within seconds, the ambulance took off, with its beacons flashing and the siren on. It looked like any other ambulance by the time it got to the end of the street but Sophia knew what was happening inside and she shut her eyes for a moment, sending out a fervent wish that they were going to be successful in saving that tiny life.

Then she opened her eyes and found herself staring at Aiden's bike.

He'd have to come back for that, wouldn't he?

Adrianna would be only too happy if Sophia hung around until Emily got back so that she could hear a first-hand account of how things had gone during transport and what was happening with the baby. It was quite reasonable to also assume that Aiden would come back with her so that he could collect his bike and get back on the road. Sophia picked up his helmet.

For a moment she held it in her arms, close to her chest. It felt like a connection to the man who'd been wearing it a short time ago. It also felt like an insurance policy. He'd have to come in to find it before he could go anywhere else. Like the way her fear had receded when Aiden had arrived at a potentially tragic scene, the knowledge that she would be able to see him again before long made everything feel a bit different.

Better?

Oh, yes... A great deal better.

But would he ask her out on another date when they actually had a chance to talk?

Their last ever date?

Her breath came out in a long, heartfelt sigh.

Maybe she didn't feel better after all.

CHAPTER TEN

Minutes turned into hours but still Aiden hadn't come back for his bike.

Sophia helped Adrianna peel a mountain of vegetables that went into the oven to roast, along with a huge leg of lamb.

'Oliver won't be far behind Em and I'm sure they're both starving. Maybe that nice young paramedic will be able to stay and have some dinner as well.'

This household was like that. A real family home where all comers were made to feel welcome.

'Wasn't he marvellous?' Adrianna added. 'It was such a relief when he arrived and even from here I could see how good he was with Ruby. A very impressive young man.'

'Mmm.' Sophia hadn't dared meet the gaze of the older woman. 'He is.'

When the front door finally opened, it was Emily's voice that could be heard.

'We're home. Sorry we were so long.'

Her tone was upbeat enough to suggest that the news was going to be good.

Adrianna came rushing from the kitchen and Sophia dropped the book she'd been reading to Toby as they cuddled on the couch.

It wasn't just Emily. Aiden was right behind her and Oliver was only a step behind them.

'Ollie gave us both a ride back,' Emily said. 'Aiden was going to get an ambulance to drop him back but when he heard that Ollie had a sixty-four Morgan sports car, he couldn't resist the invitation.'

'How did you all fit in?' Adrianna was wiping her hands on her apron.

'Bit of a squeeze,' Emily admitted, 'but we coped.' Her grin in Sophia's direction was accompanied by a ghost of a wink that suggested she hadn't minded the squeeze at all.

'I'm glad.' Adrianna smiled at Aiden. 'I hope you won't resist an invitation to stay for dinner either. I've made enough to feed an army and I want to thank you for helping our Ruby.'

'How *is* Ruby?' Sophia steadied Toby as he tried to stand up on the couch beside her, holding his arms out to his parents.

'Mumma,' he demanded.

Emily scooped him into her arms. 'Ruby's fine. No complications. She's in NICU. We couldn't persuade her to come home and get some sleep. She won't take her eyes off her daughter.'

Sophia couldn't let her breath out. She'd been too scared to ask. Her gaze shifted to Oliver. As the surgeon who'd been in charge of the in utero surgery on Ruby's baby he would be well up to date on what was happening now and he would be able to tell her. But her gaze kept travelling and only stopped when it caught Aiden's. He was smiling.

'She's doing amazingly well,' he said quietly. 'I had the privilege of being allowed to get involved while they got her settled and stable.'

'Of course you did,' Emily said. 'It was you who saved the baby in the first place.' She stepped closer to Sophia. 'You should have heard what they said about Aiden's management. He's brilliant.'

'I knew that.' It felt like her heart was in danger of bursting with pride and an odd lump in her throat made her words a little hoarse. Sophia looked back at Aiden but he seemed to be avoiding her gaze now.

'I learned a lot,' he said. 'It's not often we get to follow on with our patient's treatment like that. Luckily I've got a boss who knows how valuable it is, so I got covered for the rest of my shift.'

'You're off duty?' Adrianna beamed. 'So you can stay for dinner?'

'Well...'

'How 'bout a beer?' Oliver had taken Toby from Emily's arms to get a cuddle but now he put the small boy onto the floor. 'I think we all deserve a bit of wind-down time.'

Toby was doing his stiff-legged crawl towards his new, favourite toy.

'So that's where my helmet got to.'

'I was just looking after it,' Sophia said. 'I knew you'd come back.'

'Of course.' His gaze caught hers. And held. Sophia

could feel Emily and Oliver watching them. She knew they were both smiling and she could feel the colour creeping into her cheeks.

'For the bike,' she added.

A soft chuckle came from Adrianna, who disappeared back into the kitchen.

Aiden cleared his throat. 'I'd better ring HQ and let them know I'll be a bit late dropping it back.'

'And I'll find us a beer. A wine for you, Soph?'

'Thanks, Oliver. I'd love one.'

'Me, too,' Emily said. 'Toby, what are you doing?'

It was Aiden's turn to chuckle. 'I think he fancies riding a bike. Do you want to try that on, Toby?'

The helmet was far too big but Toby whooped with happiness when Aiden held it over his head.

'Where's my phone? I've got to get a picture of this.' Emily was laughing as she went to find it. 'Ollie, come and see. This is priceless.'

It *was* priceless. Aiden sat on the floor with Toby on his lap, wearing the helmet. All you could see was the white grin on the small, dark face. And the smile on the face of the man protecting the toddler's head from too much weight from the enormous helmet.

Something huge caught in Sophia's chest and squeezed so tightly it was hard to breathe.

Maybe it was the way Aiden was holding Toby so protectively. Or that look on his face that revealed that he was enjoying this as much as anybody else.

Or maybe it was just part of the puzzle. Another piece was that expression she'd seen when he'd been working with such determination to save Ruby's baby. How gently he'd done what had needed to be done.

And what about the first time she'd ever met this man? When he'd been holding Claire's baby boy after that emergency delivery. What had he said? Oh, yes...

'Babies are my favourite thing. It was a treat.'

Right now, toddlers seemed to be his favourite thing.

There was no question that he was more than capable of caring for and loving children. Look at the love he had for his younger brother and the way he still took responsibility for Nathan. So much so that he wasn't going to allow anything—or anyone—else to interfere with continuing to make Nathan his priority.

That was why he'd come up with that stupid three dates rule in the first place, wasn't it?

But he'd make such an amazing father.

Did he have any idea how good he would be? Was it really that he never wanted to have his own child or was he denying himself the opportunity to experience the kind of joy it could bring? Did he realise that he was shutting himself away from the chance of having a real family for himself? From having people who could support him instead of it always being the other way around?

It was actually painful to swallow the lump in her throat but Sophia managed. She even kept her tone light.

'I'll go and see if Adrianna needs some help in the kitchen.'

The kid was adorable.

The fun of the helmet wore off but Aiden apparently

had plenty of other attractions. Like the penlight torch clipped to his pocket. He showed Toby how to turn it on and it was dark enough now for the beam to show up and dance along the wall. The dog, Fuzzy, seemed to find this as good a game as Toby did. He bounced from one spot to the next, wagging his tail and barking to announce that he'd found where the light had escaped to, and this never failed to make Toby giggle with delight.

The beer hit the spot and he got the chance to talk about the in utero surgery that that tiny baby had had prior to her birth, while Emily and Sophia took Toby away for his bath. Fascinating stuff and yet his interest seemed to evaporate when the women returned. It was Sophia who was carrying Toby in his fluffy sleep suit, a bedraggled-looking toy kangaroo dangling from one hand. Sophia's cheeks were pink and her hair was a tousled mop of damp curls. And there was something about her expression that made Aiden catch his breath.

Something so tender it actually gave him a lump in his throat. When he saw the way she pressed a kiss onto Toby's head before she handed him to Oliver for a good-night cuddle, he had to turn away.

How sad was it that she would never be able to have children of her own?

To be a mother?

She'd be…amazing.

It was easy to push that disturbing sense of regret on Sophia's behalf away during the course of the delicious dinner Adrianna served up in the kitchen. There was great conversation and plenty of laughter, a dog sitting under the table in the hope of something falling his way, and an atmosphere of...what was it?

Something Aiden had never really experienced before.

Family, he realised as he reluctantly made his farewells immediately after the meal. He had to get the bike back to HQ and he'd promised Nate he'd drop in this evening so he couldn't stay any longer.

He wanted to, though.

He'd grown up in a house devoid of the kind of warmth this house was full of, and he'd pretty much lived alone ever since then. Nathan's sheltered accommodation had something of this warmth but it was very different. This was a real home—with parents and a child and a dog and even a grandma thrown in for good measure.

A real home. A real family.

Sophia looked different here. She came with him when he went to find his helmet and torch in the lounge and then saw him to the front door. Her hair was still extra-curly and there was a sparkle in her eyes that made her look extra-happy. Totally irresistible. There was nobody to witness their kiss and it was so good it would have been rude not to have another one.

She didn't just look different here. She *felt* different. Softer. More confident?

As if she was in a place where she felt completely at home?

He was even more reluctant to leave now.

'I have to go,' he murmured against her ear as he held her close. 'Nate asked me to drop in on my way home and he'll be wondering why I'm so late.'

Sophia melted out of his arms like a deflating balloon. 'Of course.'

'See you soon?'

She nodded but some of that sparkle had gone. It looked like she was holding herself very still. Holding her breath even?

'This wasn't a date.' Oh, help...why had he said that? Why bring up the fact that they only had one official date left?

Sophia didn't say anything. She smiled but she was turning away at the same time and Aiden was left with the feeling that he'd killed the sparkle completely. Pretty much like he had when he'd ruined their second date by cutting it short to go and visit his brother.

But that was precisely why he *had* to go, wasn't it?

And why he couldn't let how he felt about Sophia go any further.

It was his problem to deal with. His heart that was going to bleed when this was over.

Gunning the powerful engine of his bike gave him a momentary reprieve from the downward spiral of his mood.

He'd survive.

He'd always survived. He'd learned that long ago. Just like he'd learned how to hide how he felt so that nobody knew.

Nate knew.

He took one look at Aiden's face and his eyes narrowed. 'Man—what's up with you? Bad day?'

'No. Great day. Delivered a premmie baby. Twenty-eight-weeker. Not only that, she'd had in-utero surgery to correct spina bifida a few weeks ago, which is probably why the labour came on so early. I got to hang around in NICU while they stabilised her. You wouldn't believe some of the high-tech gear they've got in there.'

But, for once, Nathan didn't want to hear every detail of the interesting job.

'I've got something to tell you,' he said.

His tone suggested that he didn't think it would be something Aiden wanted to hear. Sudden fear made Aiden sink onto the edge of his brother's bed. What had happened? Was there something wrong that he hadn't been told about? Had Nathan's condition worsened in some way? Had he injured himself playing that fierce wheelchair rugby? Was he *sick*?

'What's the matter?' The query came out more tersely than he'd intended. 'You're not sick, are you? I hope it's not another UTI. Have you been—?'

'For God's sake,' Nathan interrupted. 'Will you stop fussing like some mother hen? No. I'm not sick. It's Sam.'

'Sam's sick?'

'No.' Nathan gave an exasperated huff of sound. 'She's not sick. She's pregnant.'

The silence fell like a brick.

Nathan shook his head. 'Don't even think about asking that one. Yeah...it's mine.'

Aiden was still too stunned to say anything. This was the last thing he'd expected to hear. Astonishment warred with something else that was even less pleasant. Fear for the challenges Nate was going to have to face? Or was it more than that? Jealousy, maybe, that there were going to be people in his brother's life who would be more important than he was? Sam. A *baby*...

'You're going to be an uncle,' Nathan told him. 'How cool is that?'

It was Aiden's turn to shake his head. 'How did that happen?'

Nathan laughed. 'You mean you don't know?' He tipped his chair, balancing on the back of the wheels. 'And you with all that medical training. Bro...'

A flash of anger surfaced. 'Cut it out, Nate. This is serious. It's not your physical capabilities I'm questioning. It's your level of intelligence in not using any kind of protection. Have you even thought about what happens next?'

The chair came down with a thump. 'What happens next is that I'm going to marry Sam. We've already applied to get a house of our own. We're going to make this work and we're very, very happy about it.' He had an odd expression on his face. 'It'd be nice if you could manage to be happy about it, too.'

'I...' Again, words failed Aiden. It felt like he was being pushed out of Nathan's life. As if the whole foundation of his own life was crumbling.

'It'll work,' Nathan said fiercely. 'I'm going to make sure it works. I can be a good dad, I know I can. And a good husband. I'm going to have a real family, Aiden, and...and I can't wait.'

You've got a family, Aiden wanted to say. *You've got me.*

But he couldn't utter the words. He knew exactly what Nathan was talking about. He'd just spent the evening with a real family, hadn't he? Did he not want that for his brother if it was possible? That kind of security?

That kind of love?

Nathan was watching him.

'It doesn't mean that I don't still need you in my life, you know.'

'I know.' The words were strangled.

But he wasn't enough. He got that but it still hurt.

'You can't make me feel guilty about this.' Nathan's words were raw. 'I know how much you've given up for me. You've felt responsible ever since the accident happened. You decided then and there you were going to be a paramedic, didn't you?'

'I guess…'

'Because you felt guilty about what happened. How many times do you have to be told, bro?' Nathan's glare was fierce. 'It. Was. Not. Your. Fault.'

'Okay…' Aiden held up his hands in a gesture of surrender. Or maybe a signal to stop. He knew that. Sophia had told him the same thing and he had—on some level—accepted it. Now Nathan was making it crystal clear that he had no choice but to let it go. To believe what everybody told him.

Sophia had done more than try to absolve his guilt. She'd thought he'd been *brave…*

'You don't get to feel guilty about me any more,'

Nathan continued. 'And that means I don't get to feel guilty about you either. Is it a deal?'

'Of course you don't get to feel guilty about me. Why would you?'

'Ooh, let me think...' Nathan shook his head. 'Maybe because you also decided you weren't going to let anything get in the way of looking after me. Anything like a pet. Or a partner. Or—heaven forbid—*kids*...'

Surely it hadn't been that obvious? It wasn't as if Aiden had even articulated what lay beneath the decisions about how he lived his life. The boundaries had simply evolved. And strengthened.

Okay, maybe he had articulated the three-dates rule. It had become a joke that was part of the bond between the brothers. He just hadn't expected Nathan to see through it with such clarity. To come to *disapprove* of it with such vehemence...

Was it because he'd fallen in love himself and was determined to make it the best relationship possible? Hurtful words spoken weeks ago drifted into his mind.

Being told that Nathan didn't want to end up like him. Shut off. Scared of losing control.

As if he was reading Aiden's mind, Nathan spoke again. The anger had gone from his voice. It was quiet now. Serious.

'We only get one life, mate, and if we don't make the best of it, we've only got ourselves to blame. You can't keep me safe because I don't want to *be* that kind of safe any more. I want to live. *Really* live. And that's what you should be doing, too.'

He reminded Aiden of Sophia saying that life wasn't

a practice run. Had he missed something along the way? Had he done the wrong thing in trying to be the best brother he could be?

'I wouldn't be where I am if it hadn't been for you,' Nathan said quietly. 'I'll love you for ever for that.'

Aiden tried to swallow the lump in his throat but it wasn't budging.

'You could have that too, you know. You and Sophia. You're perfect for each other.'

'She doesn't want that. She...she can't have kids. Doesn't want a family.'

Except that didn't really ring true, did it? Not after the way she'd looked when she'd been holding a sleepy Toby. How happy she'd been in that family kitchen.

'And you don't want kids. You've always said that being a dad to me was more than enough.'

Aiden swallowed. He had said that. He'd meant it, too. Hadn't he?

'So it's my turn to find out what it's like. You get to be the favourite uncle. Maybe Sophia would like to be an auntie. Hey, can I tell Sam it's okay to come in now? That you're not going to rain on our parade?'

'Sure.'

But Nathan hesitated at the door. 'You've got one date left with Sophia, haven't you?'

Aiden shrugged. What difference did it make?

'Make it count,' Nathan said. 'Tell her that you love her, man. It might change your life.' He grinned and his face lit up with joy. 'It changed mine.'

There were congratulations to be given after that. And plans. Not that Aiden got to say much. Nathan and

Sam seemed to have everything going just the way they wanted it to and they had the support of everybody in the house.

It was impossible not to get captured by the love these two young people had for each other. The hope that shone in their eyes as they looked at each other and shared the plans for their future.

Impossible not to come away without the realisation that he wanted that for himself, too.

That it was something worth fighting for.

It was late but maybe it wasn't *too* late.

The phone rang and rang. Any second now, and it would go to voice-mail and Aiden had no idea what he would say. Somehow he had to tell Sophia how he felt about her but you couldn't do that in a voice-mail, could you?

But then the ringing stopped and he heard Sophia's soft voice.

'Hey, Aiden...what's up?'

'Ah...' He couldn't do it over the phone either. He couldn't tell Sophia how much he loved her when he couldn't see her face. Couldn't touch her. He cleared his throat. 'I just wanted to...to...ask you out.'

'On a date?'

Oh, God...was that reluctance he could hear in her voice? A hint of fear even?

'Yeah...'

He heard what sounded like a slow, indrawn breath. 'Okay. When?'

'Um...I'm not sure. I'll text you.'

'Needs planning, huh?'

'Yeah…' He found a smile. 'The best dates always do.'

'Especially number three?' There was a catch in Sophia's voice. 'Saving the best for last?'

'Something like that. I'll text you as soon as I've got it sorted.'

It wasn't until after he'd put the phone down and started browsing his computer for ideas worthy of the perfect date that it clicked.

That reluctance.

Making it clear that this was date number three and therefore the final one.

Maybe Sophia didn't *want* it to be the final date any more than he did.

He turned back to his browsing with renewed enthusiasm.

Hope even?

The trill of her phone announcing a text came at a truly ungodly hour but Sophia woke instantly and completely as she reached to grab her mobile.

Not that she was expecting any of her women to be going into labour, but a phone call at this time of night could only signal an emergency.

Except it wasn't one of her mums-to-be.

It was an invitation for a date. If she was up for it, a taxi would be arriving to collect her in twenty minutes.

What kind of date started at four a.m.?

Certainly not a kind that Sophia had ever experienced. But, then, she'd never gone on a date knowing that it would be the last either. And she'd certainly never gone on a date with a man she was so totally and hope-lessly in love with.

Her fingers were shaking as she entered her response.

Bring it on.

CHAPTER ELEVEN

WITHOUT THE LIGHTS of the city, the night became an inky blackness surrounding the car.

Where on earth was she being taken?

Sophia had rugged up, knowing there could well be a hint of frost with the approaching dawn, but in the heat of the taxi, being wrapped in her puffer jacket and woolly accessories had her feeling drowsy.

Maybe this was all a dream?

Pulling off one woollen glove, she checked her phone. Yes. There were the text messages sent and received so recently. The last one had sent her digging through a drawer to find items of clothing that wouldn't normally make an appearance for a month or two yet.

Dress for something cold! Aiden had instructed.

Real doubt might have surfaced surrounding this date at that point but Aiden had sent another message.

Trust me.

So here she was. Speeding off in the night to an unknown destination. In a car being driven by a total stranger.

Her mother would be horrified. Sophia could almost hear an echo of her voice.

'How could you be so *reckless*, Sophia?'

A smile tilted her lips as she silently answered that voice.

Because it was Aiden who asked me, Mum. That's how.

Maybe she dozed for a while, lulled by the warmth and the rumble of the car's engine, overlaid with some easy listening music on the radio. Any minute now and she'd be hearing a track from Cat Stevens. Not that she needed the cue to think back to that evening with Aiden. To the shock of hearing about his appalling childhood. To the way his vulnerability had stolen her heart. To the understanding she had gained about why he had chosen the career he had and why he felt he had to shut anything out of his life that could get in the way of his devotion to his younger brother.

She loved him enough to know that she would never do that.

Enough to have this final date and let him go?

Yes.

But she was going to make the most of every minute of it. Especially when it had obviously been planned with great care. Like date number two. He'd taken her a long way out of the city that time, too. Was she being taken back there, perhaps? Were they going to watch the sunrise from a lighthouse overlooking one of those gorgeous beaches?

'Where *are* we going?'

'We're here, love.' The taxi driver was slowing his

vehicle, as if he was looking for a signpost. 'In the heart of the Yarra Valley.'

Nowhere near Queenscliff, then. This was pretty much the opposite direction out of Melbourne. Sophia hadn't been in this area yet but she knew it was famous for food and wine and stunning scenery.

A long way to go for a date for breakfast, though.

And the driver wasn't heading for the winery the sign had advertised. He was turning onto a side road that appeared to lead to nothing more than a big paddock beside a small lake.

Well...there was something more. A couple of trucks parked near a group of people. And a motorbike.

And someone breaking away from the group to come and meet her taxi.

Aiden had a big, puffy jacket on, too. And woolly gloves. And a beanie that covered his head and ears, but Sophia would have recognised that smile anywhere.

Her heart recognised it as well. She could feel its joyous squeeze.

'Have you guessed?' His smile widened. 'Have you ever done this before?'

Shaking her head, Sophia took hold of his hand. They were both wearing gloves but she could still feel the warmth and strength of his grip. He led her towards the huddle of people. What looked like a small house made of wicker turned out to be the bottom of a huge basket. On the other side, an enormous puddle of fabric lay on the ground.

A balloon.

This was date number three? A ride in a hot-air

balloon? How scary was this? Sophia's grip on Aiden's hand tightened. In response, he put his arm around her shoulders and pulled her firmly against his side.

You're safe, the gesture told her. *I won't let anything bad happen to you.*

Torchlight showed that the balloon had a background colour of deep gold. Big fans were positioned on either side of the basket and, as Sophia and Aiden watched, people held up the base of the fabric and air began to fill the balloon. And then, with a roar that made Sophia gasp in alarm, a huge flame emerged from the burner as someone turned it on and the air began to heat. Slowly, majestically, the balloon began to rise, tipping the basket into an upright position.

There were openings in the side of the basket and the pilot showed Aiden how to use them as footholds to climb in. Standing inside, he waited only until Sophia had her foot in the first rung and then his hands came under her arms and he lifted her as easily as if she weighed no more than a child.

And there they were, standing inside this huge basket with only the pilot for company.

'This is Jim,' Aiden told her. 'You're in safe hands.'

Sophia shook the pilot's hand. Then she looked at the ground crew, who seemed to be packing up. This was puzzling. She'd seen pictures of balloon rides like this and people were usually crammed into these baskets like human sardines.

'Haven't you got any more passengers?' she asked.

'Not today.' Jim grinned at Aiden. 'This man saved my kid's life a while back. I owed him a favour.'

Another blast of the burner punctuated his sentence and they were lifting off the ground. Aiden led her to the opposite side of the basket and pointed. Far in the distance, over the top of the Dandenong Ranges, the sun was starting to appear—a blindingly brilliant sliver of light that painted the bottoms of nearby clouds deep shades of orange and pink.

Despite the layers of clothing, it was freezing. Sophia was more than happy to be tucked against Aiden's side and each blast of the burner surrounded them with a welcome wave of warmth. It illuminated the balloon, too, and Sophia gasped with delight the first time she looked up. The dark gold of the fabric she'd seen on the ground was now a glowing, rich hue and there were patterns on it. Aboriginal designs of lizards and kangaroos and birds, and there were hand- and footprints and chains of coloured shapes filling other gaps.

'It's gorgeous.' She raised her voice to be heard over the roar of the burner but then it stopped and Aiden's response fell into complete silence.

'So are you,' he said. 'I love you, Sophia.'

Hearing Aiden say those words was like an emotional version of a burner being turned on inside her heart, lighting it up and making it glow.

The silence around them was astonishing. Somewhere down below a rooster was crowing to announce the approaching dawn but Sophia only had to whisper to be heard.

'I love you, too.'

Saying the words out loud was like a seal. The truth was out there now and it would never change. Dawn might be breaking around them to reveal stunning scenery but there was nothing she wanted to see more than what she was seeing in Aiden's eyes right now.

But it was heart-breaking, too. They loved each other but this was the last time they would be together like this. On a date.

The prickle of imminent tears made her wrench her gaze free of Aiden's. She was not going to cry in front of him. Or ruin this spectacular date he had organised. She blinked hard. Gulped in a breath of the icy air. Tried to find something to focus on. There were ponds of ground fog on the patchwork of fields and vineyards below and away in the distance she could see other balloons rising over the misty landscape. One was coloured like a rainbow. She concentrated on that, waiting for its burner to make it glow again, but it wasn't enough. She could feel a tear escape and trickle down the side of her nose.

'Oh, hon...'

Her view of the rainbow balloon vanished as Aiden gathered her into his arms. And when she raised her head all she could see was that look of love in his face. That vanished, too, as his face lowered and he kissed her.

Slowly. So tenderly her heart broke all over again.

A long blast of the burner made them finally break that kiss. Maybe the reminder that they weren't quite alone made them both look out to take in the magic of where they were, floating in the clear air of what was going to be a perfect day. There seemed to Sophia to be nothing more to say but Aiden obviously didn't think so.

'Do you remember our first date?'

'Of course. You kissed me in that garden bar.'

'Do you remember me telling you about my three-dates rule?'

Sophia nodded. How could she have forgotten? She had embraced the idea so enthusiastically. Had she really said that it was exactly the rule that was missing from her own life?

'There's something else you should know about that rule,' Aiden said softly.

'Oh?'

'Mmm.'

Aiden was staring intently at something on the ground. That flock of sheep perhaps?

'It's a load of bull.'

Sophia's jaw dropped. A loud bleating sound came from one of the sheep far below and it sounded like laughter.

'Is it...?' she managed.

Aiden straightened and met her gaze. 'It is if you find the person you want to spend the rest of your life with.' He caught her hands and gripped them tightly. 'I don't want to go on any more dates with you, Soph. I want...I want us just to be together. For ever. I want to marry you.'

'Oh...'

This was the last thing Sophia had expected to happen on this—the final—date. Had she really thought her heart had been breaking earlier? It had only been a crack. This was what it felt like to really break. To shatter into a million little pieces.

'I love you,' she whispered. 'Please, know that.' She had to close her eyes. 'But I could never marry you.'

* * *

Oh…*God*…

How devastating was this?

Aiden had planned this date knowing that his future was on the line here. That the stupid three-dates rule he'd not only invented but had given to Sophia meant that this was his last chance.

And he'd blown it.

The silence around them was deafening. Excruciating. Had Jim heard him putting his heart on the line and being turned down?

His dating rule wasn't the only stupid idea he'd ever had either. He'd chosen what seemed to be the most romantic place in the world to propose but he hadn't given any thought to failure. To being trapped in a floating box in the sky with nowhere to go. Nowhere to hide.

He would just have to grit his teeth and ride it out. To look as if he wasn't dying inside. Surely there was something out there he could focus on. Those other balloons, maybe, dotted in the sky at various levels. Yeah…there was one that had rainbow stripes. Pretty.

'It's not about the three-dates rule,' Sophia said quietly. 'It's about why you made it. About the responsibility you feel for Nate and…and how you feel about having a family.'

'I—' He had to tell her that his brother's world had changed. That his level of responsibility had been downgraded, but she didn't let him continue.

'I understand,' she told him. 'Honestly, I do. And I know that me not being able to have my own babies should make us perfect for each other but…'

He could see the way she took a deep breath. Could see the soft light that came into her eyes. 'But I *want* a family,' she said. 'And there are lots of ways of doing that without giving birth yourself.'

Aiden hadn't expected that. How arrogant had he been, assuming that Sophia had embraced the idea of limited relationships because she had no reason to want something long term when she couldn't have her own children? He had no idea what he could say to that but he didn't need to say anything yet.

Sophia's smile was poignant. 'You should know,' she said. 'Nathan is your brother, not your son, but you pretty much raised him. I love that you love him so much and it says a lot about what an amazing person you are that you've kept up that caring for him.' She scrubbed at her face with her glove as if she was wiping away a tear. Sure enough, her next words sounded choked. 'And I know it was tough. I understand why you wouldn't want to do it again.'

'I've just never considered it as an option,' Aiden put in. He needed a minute to get his head around this. Was this why Sophia couldn't marry him? Because he'd said he never wanted kids?

'I look at Emily,' Sophia said, 'and I know that that's what I want. A family. And I know it can be easier to adopt kids that aren't quite perfect and I'd be okay with that. But you've already spent your life caring for someone who needed extra help.'

'So doesn't that make me an expert?'

That surprised her into silence and it gave Aiden a moment to clear his head. To let the pieces fall into place.

Maybe it was the mention of Emily that did it. The memory of what it had been like in the Evanses' house that night. The way Sophia had looked when she'd been cuddling Toby in his fluffy sleepsuit. The laughter and warmth in that kitchen. The dog under the table.

Family.

He wanted that too, dammit.

The burst of the burner was the longest yet and it ignited something inside Aiden. Determination?

Jim's voice added a sense of urgency.

'Sorry, guys, but we're on the way down now. You'll see our chase vehicles parked up near that lake.'

Aiden didn't even look.

'The "not wanting kids" was just another stupid rule,' he told Sophia. 'Like the three-dates one. I convinced myself that's what worked because I didn't think I had the option of anything else. I felt guilty about Nate and I stuck to the promise I'd made when the accident happened. That I would look after him for ever.'

'Of course you did. Your loyalty is up there with all the other amazing things I love about you.'

'I was wrong,' Aiden insisted. 'Not about being loyal. About believing it was my fault. Nate told me but it wasn't until *you* told me that I started believing it. And now I really do. Nate and I made a deal. I'd stop feeling guilty about him and he wouldn't have to feel guilty about me.'

'He feels guilty about you?'

'He thinks I'm throwing away my own life because I think I need to look after him. He's made it very clear he's going to live his own life. He's getting married. Sam's going to have his baby.'

'Really?' Sophia sounded delighted. 'You're going to be an uncle? That's perfect for you.'

'No it's not,' Aiden growled. 'It's not enough.' He shook his head to emphasise his words. 'Yeah, I convinced myself that I didn't want anything that got in the way of putting Nate first but I did that for too long and it's a good thing that I'm not allowed to do it any more. And it means that for the first time in my life I'm going to be able to choose what *I* want. Just for myself.'

They were getting close to landing now. He could see the shadow of their balloon and its basket clearly outlined on the ground below. There was a truck parked that would carry the balloon back to its base. A car with support crew to help pack up.

Sophia wasn't looking at their shadow getting larger as the land rose to meet them. She was staring at him.

'What *do* you want?' she asked softly.

There was no hesitation on his part. 'You. Us. A family. A dog even.'

There were tears in Sophia's eyes but she was smiling. Laughing, in fact.

The bump of the basket touching the ground knocked them both off balance. A perfect excuse to take the woman he loved in his arms. To kiss her with all the joy of knowing there was hope that nothing was left to get in the way of them being together.

'That's it, folks.' Jim's voice came over what sounded like applause from the ground crew surrounding them. 'The ride's over.'

But it wasn't. Aiden couldn't keep a grin off his face as he helped Sophia from the basket and then pulled her close for another kiss.

The real ride was only just beginning.

'What happens now?' Sophia asked when he finally let her go.

The basket was on the back of the truck now and people were squashing air out of the balloon so it could be rolled up and put in its bag.

'A champagne breakfast,' he told her.

Her smile lit up the world. 'Is that a date?'

He grinned. 'Only if we have a new rule.'

'What's that? A thirty-dates rule?'

'I'm thinking more like a three-hundred-dates rule. And if that runs out, we'll make a new rule.'

Laughing, with their arms around each other, they made their way to the car that would take them to the vineyard restaurant.

'Or maybe we should make a rule about never having another date,' Aiden suggested.

'No.' Sophia tugged him to a halt and peered up at him, her bottom lip caught between her teeth as if she was trying not to smile. 'It's good that you've had so much practice because there's one date that's going to need quite a bit of planning.'

'What's that?'

'Our wedding?' Yes. The smile escaped.

Aiden's smile was coming but not quite yet. After a kiss, maybe. When that tight feeling in his chest of too much joy to handle had had a chance to subside a little.

It might need to be a long kiss, he realised as his lips captured hers.

Just as well Sophia didn't seem to mind.

* * * * *

MILLS & BOON®
Hardback – May 2015

ROMANCE

The Sheikh's Secret Babies	Lynne Graham
The Sins of Sebastian Rey-Defoe	Kim Lawrence
At Her Boss's Pleasure	Cathy Williams
Captive of Kadar	Trish Morey
The Marakaios Marriage	Kate Hewitt
Craving Her Enemy's Touch	Rachael Thomas
The Greek's Pregnant Bride	Michelle Smart
Greek's Last Redemption	Caitlin Crews
The Pregnancy Secret	Cara Colter
A Bride for the Runaway Groom	Scarlet Wilson
The Wedding Planner and the CEO	Alison Roberts
Bound by a Baby Bump	Ellie Darkins
Always the Midwife	Alison Roberts
Midwife's Baby Bump	Susanne Hampton
A Kiss to Melt Her Heart	Emily Forbes
Tempted by Her Italian Surgeon	Louisa George
Daring to Date Her Ex	Annie Claydon
The One Man to Heal Her	Meredith Webber
The Sheikh's Pregnancy Proposal	Fiona Brand
Minding Her Boss's Business	Janice Maynard

MILLS & BOON®
Large Print – May 2015

ROMANCE

The Secret His Mistress Carried	Lynne Graham
Nine Months to Redeem Him	Jennie Lucas
Fonseca's Fury	Abby Green
The Russian's Ultimatum	Michelle Smart
To Sin with the Tycoon	Cathy Williams
The Last Heir of Monterrato	Andie Brock
Inherited by Her Enemy	Sara Craven
Taming the French Tycoon	Rebecca Winters
His Very Convenient Bride	Sophie Pembroke
The Heir's Unexpected Return	Jackie Braun
The Prince She Never Forgot	Scarlet Wilson

HISTORICAL

Marriage Made in Money	Sophia James
Chosen by the Lieutenant	Anne Herries
Playing the Rake's Game	Bronwyn Scott
Caught in Scandal's Storm	Helen Dickson
Bride for a Knight	Margaret Moore

MEDICAL

Playing the Playboy's Sweetheart	Carol Marinelli
Unwrapping Her Italian Doc	Carol Marinelli
A Doctor by Day...	Emily Forbes
Tamed by the Renegade	Emily Forbes
A Little Christmas Magic	Alison Roberts
Christmas with the Maverick Millionaire	Scarlet Wilson

0415 GEN STD LP

MILLS & BOON®
Hardback – June 2015

ROMANCE

The Bride Fonseca Needs	Abby Green
Sheikh's Forbidden Conquest	Chantelle Shaw
Protecting the Desert Heir	Caitlin Crews
Seduced into the Greek's World	Dani Collins
Tempted by Her Billionaire Boss	Jennifer Hayward
Married for the Prince's Convenience	Maya Blake
The Sicilian's Surprise Wife	Tara Pammi
Russian's Ruthless Demand	Michelle Conder
His Unexpected Baby Bombshell	Soraya Lane
Falling for the Bridesmaid	Sophie Pembroke
A Millionaire for Cinderella	Barbara Wallace
From Paradise...to Pregnant!	Kandy Shepherd
Midwife...to Mum!	Sue MacKay
His Best Friend's Baby	Susan Carlisle
Italian Surgeon to the Stars	Melanie Milburne
Her Greek Doctor's Proposal	Robin Gianna
New York Doc to Blushing Bride	Janice Lynn
Still Married to Her Ex!	Lucy Clark
The Sheikh's Secret Heir	Kristi Gold
Carrying A King's Child	Katherine Garbera

MILLS & BOON®
Large Print – June 2015

ROMANCE

The Redemption of Darius Sterne	Carole Mortimer
The Sultan's Harem Bride	Annie West
Playing by the Greek's Rules	Sarah Morgan
Innocent in His Diamonds	Maya Blake
To Wear His Ring Again	Chantelle Shaw
The Man to Be Reckoned With	Tara Pammi
Claimed by the Sheikh	Rachael Thomas
Her Brooding Italian Boss	Susan Meier
The Heiress's Secret Baby	Jessica Gilmore
A Pregnancy, a Party & a Proposal	Teresa Carpenter
Best Friend to Wife and Mother?	Caroline Anderson

HISTORICAL

The Lost Gentleman	Margaret McPhee
Breaking the Rake's Rules	Bronwyn Scott
Secrets Behind Locked Doors	Laura Martin
Taming His Viking Woman	Michelle Styles
The Knight's Broken Promise	Nicole Locke

MEDICAL

Midwife's Christmas Proposal	Fiona McArthur
Midwife's Mistletoe Baby	Fiona McArthur
A Baby on Her Christmas List	Louisa George
A Family This Christmas	Sue MacKay
Falling for Dr December	Susanne Hampton
Snowbound with the Surgeon	Annie Claydon

0515 GEN STD LP

MILLS & BOON®

Why shop at millsandboon.co.uk?

Each year, thousands of romance readers find their perfect read at millsandboon.co.uk. That's because we're passionate about bringing you the very best romantic fiction. Here are some of the advantages of shopping at www.millsandboon.co.uk:

* **Get new books first**—you'll be able to buy your favourite books one month before they hit the shops

* **Get exclusive discounts**—you'll also be able to buy our specially created monthly collections, with up to 50% off the RRP

* **Find your favourite authors**—latest news, interviews and new releases for all your favourite authors and series on our website, plus ideas for what to try next

* **Join in**—once you've bought your favourite books, don't forget to register with us to rate, review and join in the discussions

Visit **www.millsandboon.co.uk**
for all this and more today!